D1002188

Fiction Notho.A

Nothomb, Amelie.

The character of rain /

THE CHARACTER
OF RAIN

THE CHARACTER
OF RAIN

AMÉLIE NOTHOMB

Translated by Timothy Bent

St. Martin's Press ✹ New York

www.stmartins.com

Translation of extract from poem by Louis Aragon on pages 68-69 by Timothy Bent.

Library of Congress Cataloging-in-Publication Data

Nothomb, Amélie
[Metaphysique des tubes. English]
The character of rain : a novel / Amélie Nothomb ; translated by Timothy Bent
p. cm.
ISBN 0-312-28600-7
I. Bent, Timothy. II Title.

PQ2674.O778 M4813 2002
843'.914—dc21 2001048998

First published in France under the title *Métaphysique des tubes* by Editions Albin Michel S.A.

First U.S. Edition: April 2002

10 9 8 7 6 5 4 3 2 1

THE CHARACTER
OF RAIN

IN THE BEGINNING was nothing, and this nothing had neither form nor substance—it was nothing other than what it was. And God knew that it was good. God would not have created something other than nothing for anything in the world, for it did more than merely please, it fulfilled.

God's eyes were perpetually wide open and staring, though it didn't matter whether they were opened or closed. There was nothing to see, and God, plump and compact as a hard-boiled egg, saw nothing.

God was absolute satisfaction—wanting nothing, expecting nothing, perceiving nothing, rejecting nothing, interested in nothing. So complete was life at this stage that it wasn't life. God didn't live, simply existed.

There had been no noticeable starting point to existence. Great books have beginnings we forget immediately; they make us feel we have been reading them since the dawn of time. So, too, it was impossible to mark the moment at which God had started to exist.

God did not have language and therefore did not have thought. All was fullness and eternity, establishing beyond all doubt that God was God. Not that this mattered. God cared nothing about being God.

■ ■ ■

THE EYES OF LIVING CREATURES possess that most astounding of all capacities: sight. Nothing is more unique.

What sight means cannot be expressed. Words can't capture its strange essence. Yet sight exists, and in a way that few other things do.

There is a profound difference between eyes with sight and eyes without sight. That difference has a name: life. Life begins with sight.

God had no sight.

■ ■ ■

GOD'S SOLE PREOCCUPATIONS were ingestion, digestion, and, as a direct result, excretion. These vegetative activities took place without God's even being aware of them. Nourishment, always the same, wasn't exciting enough to take much note of. God simply opened all the appropriate orifices for it to pass in, and through, and out.

That is why at this stage of its development we shall call God "the Tube."

There have been theories about tubes, and for good reason: they are singular combinations of fullness and emptiness; they are hollow substance, a something that contains nothing. Tubes can be flexible, but it renders them no less mysterious.

God's body was supple yet inert, thus confirming its total absorption in cylindrical serenity—filtering everything in the universe, retaining nothing.

THE PARENTS OF THE TUBE were deeply concerned. They brought specialists in to examine the strange case of this lifeless length of living tissue.

The specialists tested the Tube's articulations, tapping knees and elbows to determine whether there was a reflexive response, which there wasn't. Nor did the Tube's pupils move when they shined a light directly into them.

"The child never cries, and never moves. Never makes a sound," the parents told the doctors.

They concluded that here was a case of "pathological apathy," apparently unaware this was a contradiction in terms.

"Your child is a vegetable. It is most upsetting."

Actually, the parents were relieved by their diagnosis. A vegetable, after all, is still a living thing.

"She should be put in the hospital," said the specialists.

The parents ignored the advice. They already had two children who were full-fledged members of the human race. Having a third who was a vegetable wasn't so bad. It even elicited tender feelings on their part.

They sweetly called the Tube "the Plant."

　　■　■　■

CALLING THE TUBE "the Plant," however, was a case of mistaken identity. For all that they lead a life imperceptible to the human eye, plants, including vegetables, are alive. They tremble when a storm approaches, weep bitter tears at break of day, are indignant when attacked, and go crazy with ecstasy—launching themselves into the dance of the seven veils—during the pollen season. Without doubt they see things, though where their eyes are located no one knows.

The Tube, on the other hand, was wholly and completely impassive. Nothing affected it—not changes in temperature, not nightfall, not the hundreds of daily emotions and mood swings, not the great and inexplicable mysteries of silence.

The monthly earthquakes, which caused its older siblings to cry out in fear, had no effect whatever on the Tube. The Richter Scale was a measurement for others, not for the Tube. One evening, a tremor measuring 5.6 shook the mountain on which their house sat. Pieces of plaster rained down on the Tube's cradle. When they took it out, the Tube was indifference itself, its eyes fixed upon, but not seeing, those who had come to disturb it from under the pile of debris, where it had been warm.

The parents were determined to find out everything they could about the Plant and decided to try an experiment. They stopped giving it food and drink. Finally, they thought, the child would be forced to react.

The plan backfired. The Tube accepted starvation the way it accepted everything else—without a shadow of disapproval or resentment. Eating or not eating, drinking or not drinking, it was all the same. To be or not to be was not the question.

At the end of the third day, the parents, wild with worry, examined their little Plant. It had gotten a little thinner and its lips were parched, but it didn't seem much worse off than before. They gave the Tube a bottle with sugar water, which it drank in without emotion.

"This child would let itself die without complaining," said the mother, horrified.

"Let's not tell the doctors," said the father. "They'd think we were sadists."

The parents were not sadists; they were simply stunned to discover that their issue lacked any instinct for survival. It crossed their minds that their baby wasn't a plant but a tube, but they instantly rejected such an idea as unthinkable.

It was in the nature of the parents to be happy, and soon they forgot all about their little experiment. They had three children: a boy, a girl, and a vegetable. The diversity pleased them, all the more because the older children were forever running around, crying, fighting, jumping, and inventing new games. They needed to be watched constantly.

Their youngest child didn't cause them any such worries. They could leave it for entire days without a babysitter. In the evening they would find it in exactly the same position they had left it in the morning. They changed its diaper, gave it some nourishment, and that was pretty much all there was to it. A goldfish would have been more trouble.

Moreover, aside from the fact that it didn't seem to have sight, the Tube looked like a normal baby, the kind you could show off to guests without embarrassment. Other parents were even jealous.

In truth, it was the incarnation of inertia, the strongest yet most paradoxical of all forces, emanating from something that doesn't move. When a body goes limp, when a car pushed by ten strong men refuses to budge, when a child lies in a heap in front of the TV for hours and hours, and when an inane idea continues to exert its noxious influence, one confronts the numbing, terrifying grip of inertia.

Such was the power of the Tube.

* * *

IT NEVER CRIED. It did not wail at the moment of its birth, nor even uttered a sound. The world was not worth bothering about.

The mother had tried breastfeeding. No instinct impelled the baby's mouth toward the maternal pap; baby and breast were put nose to nose, but the newborn didn't attempt to move closer. The mother, concerned and irritated, had forced her nipple into its mouth. God sucked barely, if at all. The mother decided to feed it from a bottle.

The bottle corresponded far better to her child's essential nature. Mammary roundness had not inspired the tiniest feeling of filial attachment, but the Tube took immediately to this cylindrical source of nourishment.

Thus the mother fed the child several times a day, innocent of the fact that she was reinforcing the connection between tubes. Divine alimentation was something akin to plumbing.

* * *

"ALL IS FLUX," "nothing endures but change," "you could not step twice into the same river." So said Heraclitus. The ancient philosopher would have been driven to despair had he met the Tube, who was the very negation of his fluid vision of the universe. Had the Tube been capable of language, it would have replied to this venerable sage: "All is static," "everything endures," "you always step into the same river," and so on.

Luckily, language isn't possible without movement, without some kind of engine driving it, and thought isn't possible without language. The Tube's metaphysical speculations were neither thinkable nor communicable, and therefore couldn't do any harm. This was a good thing, for otherwise they would have sapped humanity's morale for a very long time.

＊　＊　＊

GOD'S PARENTS WERE of Belgian nationality, meaning that it, too, was Belgian. This may help explain not a few of the disasters that have occurred since biblical days; centuries ago, a priest from the Low Countries proved scientifically that Adam and Eve spoke Flemish.

The Tube, however, had found an ingenious solution to humanity's post-Babel linguistic difficulties: it never produced even the smallest sound.

The muteness concerned the parents less than the

immobility. The child reached the age of one year without having twitched a muscle. Other children were taking their first steps, making their first smiles, doing their first whatevers. Theirs hadn't accomplished a single thing.

This was all the more strange because the Tube was developing in ways that were otherwise absolutely normal. The brain simply wasn't keeping pace. The parents regarded this growth process with perplexity, for their house was being inhabited by a void that nonetheless took up more and more space.

The cradle became too small. The Tube was transplanted to a crib, the same one used previously by its older brother and sister.

"Maybe moving the Plant will wake it up," said the mother, sighing.

It didn't.

From the beginning of the universe, God had slept in the same room as its parents. This didn't pose problems for them, of course. They could forget it was even there.

*   *   *

TIME, LIKE LANGUAGE, is a product of movement. Not moving, the Tube had no awareness of time's passage. Eventually it turned two, though it might as well have turned two days, or two centuries for that matter. It had neither changed positions nor attempted to; it remained, as ever, on its back, arms at its side, like a tiny effigy.

One day the mother lifted the Plant by its shoulders to set it on its feet; the father put its tiny hands on the side of the crib, and encouraged it to grip. Then they let go. It instantly tumbled backward and contentedly resumed its former position.

"Maybe music would help," the mother suggested. "Children respond to music."

Mozart, Chopin, the soundtrack from *101 Dalmatians,* Beatles songs, *Shaku hachi*—all of them elicited precisely the same reaction: none.

The parents gave up trying to make it into a musician. By this point they had given up trying to make it human.

* * *

SEEING INVOLVES CHOICE. Whoever looks at something has decided to fix his attention on that one thing, to the exclusion of other things. That is why sight, the very essence of life, first and foremost constitutes a rejection.

Therefore, to live means to reject. Anyone who looks at everything at once is as alive as a toilet bowl. Living means making a distinction between, for example, the mother and the ceiling—things that are overhead. One must choose to be interested in one or the other, either the mother or the ceiling. The only wrong choice is the absence of choice.

God hadn't refused because it hadn't made a choice. That was why it wasn't alive.

When babies are born, their howl of pain is, in and of itself, a revolt; and a revolt is, in and of itself, a rejection. Hence life begins on the day of birth—not before, as some believe.

God had not emitted a single sound, of course, not the faintest decibel since the second it emerged from the mother's womb. Yet the specialists had determined it was not deaf, nor blind, nor dumb. It was like a sink without a stopper. Had it been able to speak, it would have endlessly repeated the same word—"yes."

* * *

HUMANITY HAS FORMED a cult around normalcy. We want to believe that our evolution was the result of a natural and normal process, that our species has been guided by a biological inevitability that led us, after many millennia, to stop crawling at the age of one and begin moving upright.

We prefer not to believe in accidents, for they are expressions either of an exterior force, which is bothersome enough, or of pure chance, which is worse, and hence banished from our thoughts. Were someone to dare utter, "I took my first steps about the age of one by accident," or, "man became bipedal by accident," he would be considered a lunatic.

The accident theory is unacceptable because it permits thinking that things didn't have to turn out the way they have. People can't conceive of the notion that an infant doesn't want to talk. It would be like admitting that man might never have gotten the idea of walking upright. A gifted species as ours might never have thought of walking upright? Unthinkable.

By the age of two, the Tube hadn't attempted to crawl, nor even made a move in that direction. Nor, still, made a peep. The adults—the parents, the doctors, and the nanny—decided there must be some kind of developmental blockage. It would never have occurred to them that what was wrong with the child might not be physical in nature, for who could have believed that, barring some accident of fate, man might have preferred to remain as inert as a larva?

There are, of course, physical accidents and mental accidents. People dismiss the latter out of hand as far as evolution goes.

Yet nothing could be more fundamental to the human story than mental accidents. At some point, deep in the past, a particle of grit lodged itself in an oyster. Suddenly the tender, oozy matter inside the shell felt violated by this tiny foreign element that had penetrated its defenses. The oyster, which had been vegetating quite happily really, sounded the alarm and closed ranks. It invented a marvelous new substance, nacre, to surround the offending particle, thereby inventing the pearl.

A mental accident can also befall the brain from within. These are the most mysterious and serious of all. For no apparent reason, a particular circumlocution of the gray matter gives birth to the grain of a horrific thought—a truly terrifying thought—and in a flash well-being has disappeared.

The virus goes to work. The infection forces the creature out of its torpor, assailing it with a question to which it must formulate a thousand replies. It starts to walk, to speak, and to assume a hundred wholly futile attitudes by which it hopes to escape.

Not only does all this activity not help, it makes matters worse. The more the creature talks the less it understands, the more it walks the more ground it has to cover. Soon it starts to miss its former, peaceful, larval state, but without daring to admit this.

There are those who have not been subjected to the laws of evolutionary development. These are the clinical vegetables. The specialists fret over them. Yet they are what we want to be. They are experiencing life as it would have been lived but for a fateful accident.

AN ORDINARY DAY. The parents were acting like parents, the other children were behaving like children, and the Tube was wrapped up in its cylindrical existence.

Nonetheless, this day would be the most important day of its life, then disappear without a trace, just as there apparently are no remains of that day when a human being rose to his feet for the first time, nor the day when he first grasped what death truly meant. The pivotal events in mankind's history happen without notice.

Anyway, on this ordinary day, the walls of the house suddenly echoed with screams. Terrified, the mother and the nanny ran from room to room in search of its source. Had a monkey gotten loose? Had someone escaped from an insane asylum?

The last place the mother looked was her room. What she saw froze her in her tracks. The Plant was sitting up in its crib, howling as only a two-year-old child can howl.

The mother approached the crib, trying to reconcile this ear-splitting spectacle with the image of what, for two long years, had been the embodiment of placidity. The Plant's eyes had always been opened wide and staring fixedly, their gray-green color therefore easy to identify; now its pupils were entirely black, black as a scorched field.

What force had been so powerful as to turn those pale eyes into coals? What dreadful thing could have happened to it?

The only clear thing was that the child was furious— seized up in a fabulous fit of rage.

Fascinated, the mother took her child in her arms, but the child kicked wildly and she put it straight back down.

She ran through the house, yelling, "The Plant isn't a plant!" She called to her husband. He ran to their room. The brother and sister were invited in to witness the splendor of such divine fury.

After a while, the child stopped howling, though its eyes remained menacingly dark. Seething with anger, it regarded the humanity assembled around it. Then, exhausted, it lay down and fell asleep.

The family began to applaud. They were over-joyed. The child had at long last come to life.

．　．　．

THE SPECIALISTS COULDN'T explain this sudden rebirth. It was as if, they said, the child needed two full years of extrauterine womblike existence to become operational.

As for the rage, the only explanation advanced was that it was the product of a mental event. Something had happened in its brain, something it couldn't accommodate, and instantaneously the gray matter had been shaken out of its slumber. Neural messages had begun coursing through the nervous system. The body started to move.

Great empires can collapse for reasons that initially seem perfectly incomprehensible.

Children as still as statues can suddenly turn into braying beasts. The most surprising thing was how much this delighted the family.

Sic transit tubi gloria.

The father couldn't get over his excitement. He felt as if he had a newborn. He called his mother, who lived in Brussels.

"The Plant woke up! Get on a plane and come right away!"

The grandmother replied that she would need to

have a couple of suits made before coming all the way to Japan, which is where her son and his family were living. She was a most elegant woman. The suits would take at least a month or two.

In the meantime, the parents began to miss their Plant. Having awoken in a rage, their child had remained constantly enraged. The mother or the nanny nearly had to throw a bottle into its crib, then back away quickly before getting whacked. There were moments—sometimes lasting for hours—when the child was calm, but these were pre-storm calms. They would take advantage of one of these quiet moments and take the child out into the yard, where it sat on the grass, contemplating the toys placed around it.

God—no longer "the Tube" or "the Plant," it was still the center of the universe—would slowly grow upset, realizing that these toys existed outside of it, that their existence was not dependent. This caused profound displeasure.

Nonetheless, it had not escaped God's notice that those around it produced precise, articulated sounds with their mouths, and that somehow these sounds enabled them to control objects, to annex them.

It wanted to do that. Was it not a divine prerogative to name all things in the universe? God therefore designated an object with its finger and opened its mouth to speak, but the sounds that came out were incoherent. God was the first to find this surprising; it felt completely capable of speech. The surprise diminished, replaced by feelings of humiliation and outrage. Then the screaming started.

The meaning of its screaming was as follows:

They move their lips and words come out. God moves its lips and all that comes out is noise. This is not fair. It will yell and scream until noise turns into language.

Here was how the mother interpreted what was happening:

Acting like a baby at the age of two isn't normal. The child must sense that she is late to develop and that's why she gets mad.

The mother's conclusion was false. God did not believe God to be late. To say such a thing suggested a comparison, and God wouldn't submit to comparisons. It sensed within itself enormous power, and was frustrated to discover that it was incapable of exercising that power. The mouth betrayed it. The lips weren't up to the task.

The mother approached the child, speaking in a loud voice that stretched out every syllable:

"Paaaapaaaa! Maaaamaaaa!"

God was infuriated that anyone would propose imitating such inanities. Did the mother not know she was dealing with a master of language, one who would never debase itself by repeating "mama" and "papa"? In response to the mother's overtures the child launched into full-throated howling more hideous than ever.

Little by little the parents began to talk openly about what the child had been like before. Was this really such an improvement? Once they had had a child who was mysteriously and wonderfully placid, and now they had a pit bull pup on their hands.

"Do you remember how pretty the Plant was? Those large peaceful eyes."

"We slept so well in those days."

There was no more rest for the parents. God was an insomniac, sleeping barely an hour or two a night. When it wasn't sleeping, it was screaming.

"That's enough!" the father would shout at the crib. "We know you spent two years snoozing. That's not a reason to keep us up!"

God behaved like Louis XIV: unable to tolerate the idea that anyone would sleep when it wasn't, eat when it wasn't, or talk when it couldn't. This last one really got it spitting mad.

The specialists were no more successful at explaining this behavior than they had been before. "Pathological apathy" became "pathological irritability" without any hard proof. In the end, they fell back upon common sense:

"She's compensating for the two years she missed. She'll quiet down eventually."

If I haven't thrown her out the window by then, thought the exasperated mother.

. . .

WITH TIME THE GRANDMOTHER'S SUITS were made. She packed them into a suitcase, went to the hairdresser's, and took a plane from Brussels to Osaka. In those days the flight took twenty hours.

The parents were waiting at the airport. They hadn't seen her in three years. She embraced her son, congratulated her daughter-in-law, and pronounced Japan wonderful.

On the drive into the mountains the parents talked about the children. The two older ones were marvelous; the youngest was a problem. "It's almost more than we can take," they admitted. The grandmother assured them that everything would work out.

Their house enchanted her. "It's so Japanese!" she exclaimed, looking at the *tatami* room and the garden, which, though this was February, was filled with plum trees in bloom.

The grandmother hadn't seen the children in three years, and was delighted to find that the little boy was already seven and the little girl five. She then asked to be introduced to the third child, whom she had never seen at all.

The parents were hesitant to lead her into the monster's lair. "It's on the second floor, the first room on the left. You can't miss it." They could already hear raucous howls. The grandmother took something out of her travel bag and marched stalwartly into the arena.

*   *   *

TWO AND A HALF YEARS. Cries, rage, hate. The world was beyond the hands and voice of God. Encircled by bars, it wanted to destroy everything and couldn't, so it took revenge out on the sheet and blankets, hammering at them with its heels.

God knew by heart the cracks in the ceiling. They were its only companions, and it was at them that it screamed abuse. The ceiling seemed unaffected, and this infuriated God all the more.

Suddenly its field of vision was filled with an unfamiliar face. An adult, of the same kind as the mother, from the look of her. After the moment of surprise had passed, God expressed its displeasure with a bloodcurdling yowl.

The face smiled. God knew what she was trying to do. Pacify it. This would not work. It bared its teeth.

The face let some words drop from its mouth. God slapped them away.

God knew that subsequently this adult would extend her hand. Adults always approached its face with their fingers. It prepared to bite.

And indeed the hand approached, but it was holding something unexpected—something unknown—in its fingers. A white stick. God had not seen such a thing before and forgot about biting.

"This," said the grandmother to the child, "is white chocolate from Belgium."

The only word that God recognized was "white." Walls were white, milk was white. The others were obscure—"chocolate" and "Belgium." Pondering these indecipherable sounds, it realized that the stick was near its mouth.

"It's for eating," said the voice.

"Eating." A known word. Something it did often. Eating was the bottle, carrot puree with small bits of meat, crushed banana with chunks of apple.

Eating involved familiar smells. The odor of this white stick was unrecognizable—but better than soap and applesauce. God was afraid and tempted at the same time. It made a grimace of disgust yet salivated with desire.

In a leap of faith God took this new thing with its

teeth, and was going to bite down hard except doing so turned out not to be necessary, for the strange white substance melted on the tongue, and instantly took command of the mouth.

Sweetness rose to God's head and tore at its brain, forcing out a voice it had never before heard:

It is I! I'm talking! I'm not an "it" I'm a "me"! You can no longer say "it" when you talk about yourself. You have to say "me." And I am your best friend. I'm the one who gives you pleasure.

And thus it was that I was born in Japan at the age of two and a half, in February of 1970, in the province of Kansai, in the village of Shukugawa, under the benevolent gaze of my paternal grandmother, and by the grace of her white chocolate.

The voice has never died since that day, and it still speaks in my head.

Yum, that's good. It's sweet and smooth, and I want more of it.

I took another bite of the white stick and moaned.

Pleasure is a wonderful thing, for it has taught me that I am me. Me: where pleasure is. Pleasure is me. Wherever there is pleasure there is me. No pleasure without me. No me without pleasure!

Mouthful by mouthful, the stick disappeared. The voice inside my head started to shout louder and louder.

Hooray for me! I am as powerful as the sweetness that I can taste and which I invented. Without me, this chocolate would be nothing. But when you put it in my mouth it becomes pleasure. It needs me.

This thought was translated in my head by shattering explosions of delight. I opened my enormous eyes and kicked my legs, but this time in glee. Images, sensations, thoughts were impressing themselves on my brain, which retained every detail.

Piece by piece the chocolate became part of me. I grew dimly aware that at the end of this delectable thing of infinite sweetness was a hand, and that at the end of this hand was a person, and that this person was smiling. The voice inside me spoke again.

I don't know who you are, but because you brought me something wonderful to eat you must be kind.

The two arms attached to the hands lifted me out of my crib and bore me aloft.

■ ■ ■

MY PARENTS WERE STUNNED to see my grandmother arrive, still smiling, carrying a docile and contented child in her arms.

"I'd like to introduce you to my new friend," she announced with triumph.

I let myself be passed from arm to arm. My mother and father couldn't believe my metamorphosis—and were both thrilled and irritated. They asked my grandmother how she had performed this miracle.

My grandmother didn't tell them about the white chocolate. She preferred that it remain her secret. The parents wondered whether she had performed some kind of exorcism. None of them could have guessed that I knew exactly what had happened.

Bees feed honey to larvae to give them an appetite for life. Pureed carrots with small bits of meat wouldn't have worked. My mother had her theories about sugar, which, she felt, was responsible for most of the world's ills. Yet this "poison" (as she termed it) had made her third child fit for society.

I knew myself, and I soon discovered that life was a vale of tears in which one was forced to eat pureed carrots with small bits of meat. It was such a disappointment. Why go to all the trouble of being born if not to experience pleasure? Adults have access to all kinds of wonderful things, but for children the only true pleasure lies in eating. That is the key that opens doors.

My grandmother had filled my mouth with sugar, and suddenly the feral creature that I was understood that there was some justification to boredom, that the body and the spirit existed to exult in pleasures, and that there was no reason to despise the world nor oneself for joining it. Pleasure used its occasion to name its instrument: it called it "me"—a name I have kept all these years.

There has always been a large group of imbeciles opposing sensuality to intelligence. They inhabit a vicious circle: they deny themselves any extravagance to exalt their intellect, and the result is they diminish their intellect. They grow more and more dull, which leads them to become more and more convinced they are brilliant. There is no greater purpose for stupidity than to believe itself brilliant.

Pleasure renders us humble, admiring of the thing that has made pleasure possible. It awakens the spirit and pushes it to both greater heights and greater depths. The magical thing is that the idea of pleasure by itself will suffice. From the very second pleasure exists for us, existence is salvaged. Self-denial condemns itself to celebrating only its own nothingness.

There are people who boast of having done without some luxury for twenty-five years. There are fools who glory in never having listened to music, or read a book, or seen a movie. There are those who seek praise for their chastity. Such vanity is necessary. It provides them with the only pleasure they get from being alive.

BY GIVING ME AN IDENTITY, the white chocolate had also provided me, as I've said, with a memory. I remember everything after February of 1970. There isn't any point to remembering that which has no connection to pleasure. Memory is one of luxury's most indispensable allies.

A statement of those proportions—"I remember everything after February of 1970"—stands little chance of being believed. I don't particularly care. It can't be either proved or disproved, so I'm less and less interested in being believed.

Of course, I don't remember all my parents' worries, or every conversation they had with their friends, or much of that sort. But I have forgotten nothing essential: the greenness of the lake in which I learned to swim, the smell of the garden, the taste of the plum wine I sipped when no one was watching.

Before the white chocolate, I remember nothing, and am forced to rely on what others tell me, then filter their recollections through my mind. But after the white chocolate, everything I know I remember first-hand—the same hand writing this.

* * *

I BECAME THE KIND OF CHILD that parents dream of. I was alert but judicious, silent but present, funny but thoughtful, high-spirited but attentive, obedient but independent.

My grandmother and her goodies remained in Japan for only a month, but this was long enough. The very idea of pleasure had set me into motion. My father and mother were greatly relieved. Having had a vegetable for two years and a wild beast for six months, they finally had a child who was more or less normal. They started calling me by my first name.

What was necessary now was to make up for lost time (though I didn't think I had lost it). At two and a half a human must walk and talk. I started by walking, which is how things generally happen. There isn't any magic to it. You stand up, let yourself pitch forward, place your weight on one foot, then on the other.

There was undeniable value to walking. It afforded a far better view of things than did crawling. Walking inevitably led to running, and running was a wonderful discovery, for it made evasion possible. One could make off with some forbidden object without being seen. Running allowed naughtiness to go unpunished. It was the operative verb for highway robbers and warriors and heroes.

Talking, on the other hand, posed certain problems of etiquette. Which word should I utter first? I could easily have chosen "ice cream" or "peepee," or something as beautiful as "tire" or "Scotch," but none of these seemed quite right.

Parents are vulnerable creatures; they need to hear the old standbys to make them feel secure. Secrecy was also imperative. I didn't want to say anything that would give too much away. Therefore, with a solemn and dignified bearing, I said out loud for the first time one of the sounds inside my head.

"Mama!"

Ecstatic mother.

And, as I didn't want to upset the delicate balance of things, I quickly added,

"Papa!"

Father dissolved in tenderness.

My parents scooped me up and showered me with kisses. All I could think was how simple they were, really. They would have been less delighted had I started out with something along the lines of, "There are snakes hissing on your heads" or, "all is in flux." It was as if they doubted their own identity. Weren't they already sure enough of being my mother and father without me calling them "Mama" and "Papa"? They seemed to need me to confirm their roles in life.

However, all in all, I was pleased with my choices. No first words could have given my begetters greater satisfaction. I had also fulfilled my obligation to family life. The whole issue of the third word was deeply exciting. I had maintained the family hierarchy, and now was free to turn to other matters. This freedom was so daunting that for a very long time I didn't utter that third word, which flattered my parents even more. "She only needed to name us. We are her greatest necessity."

They didn't know that inside my head I had been talking for some quite some time. Saying something out loud is different, however. It confers an exceptional value on the word spoken. It lends the word weight, gives it life, recognition, as if you're repaying a debt to it, or celebrating its essence. To say the word "banana" is to offer homage to all the bananas that have existed across the centuries.

I thought very hard about what to say next, beginning a phase of intense intellectual exploration that went on for weeks. Photos taken of me during this period show me looking so preoccupied as to seem comic. This was because of the inner dialogue in which I was engaged. "Shoe"? Not important enough; you could walk without it. "Paper"? Yes, but a pencil was just as important, and choosing between the two would have been impossible. "Chocolate?" No, that was a secret. "Sea lion"? Sea lions were wonderful and always elicited burbles of delight, but were they really better than, say, a top? Tops were wonderful, too. But sea lions were alive. Which was better, a spinning top or a living sea lion? The inability to decide made me choose neither. "Harmonica"? It sounded nice, but was it really necessary? "Glasses"? They were funny, but didn't serve any purpose I could see. "Xylophone?" And so it went.

One day my mother came into the living room pulling a creature by its elongated neck and attaching its long, thin tail to a wall. She pushed a button and the beast sputtered to life with a loud, plaintive whine. The head started to move on the ground, backward and forward, pushing my mother's arm with it. Sometimes the body moved on paws that were actually wheels.

This was not the first time I had seen a vacuum cleaner, but it was the first time I had truly considered it. I approached it on all fours so as to put myself at its level.

I knew that it was always necessary to examine objects at their own level. I followed the movement of its head and rested my cheek on the rug to see what happened. The result was miraculous: the thing swallowed up the little things that it came upon and made them disappear.

It therefore replaced something with nothing—an act that could only be divine in origin.

I had the vague idea of having been God, and not very long before. A loud voice in my head sometimes plunged me into a deep reverie. *Remember, I live inside you! Remember!* I didn't know what I thought about this, though the idea of my divinity seemed both probable and pleasing.

Now suddenly I had a brother: the vacuum. What could be more divine than this pure annihilator of material things? God had to have such power.

Anch'io sono pittore! Correggio was said to have exclaimed when he first discovered Raphael's paintings. Matching that enthusiasm, I was on the point of crying out, "I'm a vacuum, too!" but at the last second remembered that I needed to be careful. I was thought to be in command of two words. Suddenly uttering a complete sentence wouldn't do. At least I had found my third word. Opening my mouth, I produced the requisite syllables.

"Vacuum!"

My mother immediately let go of the neck and ran to the phone.

"Guess what?" she asked my father. "She's just said her third word!"

"What is it?"

" 'Vacuum!' "

"Well, maybe she'll grow up to be a first-class maid."

He was obviously a little disappointed.

I had gone all out for that third word, and decided that I could allow myself to be a little less philosophical when it came to the fourth. I decided that naming my sister, who was two and a half years older than I, would be the right thing to do.

"Juliette!" I exclaimed, looking into her eyes.

What power language had! The very second I said her name we were all over each other. My sister took me in her arms and held me tight. Her name, stronger than Tristan and Isolde's love elixir, bonded us for life.

As far as the fifth word went, pronouncing my brother's name was out of the question. He was four years older than I, and had once spent an entire afternoon reading his Tintin comic while sitting on my head. He loved to torture me. To punish him, I decided he would remain unnamed. He therefore didn't truly exist.

Nishio-san was my Japanese nanny. She was goodness itself and devoted herself to me with endless patience. She spoke only Japanese, but I understood everything she said. My fifth word was her name.

I had therefore given names to four people. Each time, I had made them so happy that no longer could I question the importance of words. The proof was that these people were there. I concluded that they had needed me to help them exist.

Did that mean that speaking gave life? This was far from clear, I thought. People around me spoke from morning to night, and their words often produced neither monumental nor even discernible results. With my parents, for example, speaking could involve something like the following:

"I invited the Whatstheirnames for the twenty-sixth."

"Who are the Whatstheirnames?"

"Oh come on, Danièle, you know very well who they are. We've only had dinner with them twenty times."

"I still don't remember. Who are they again?"

"You'll see."

I did not get the impression that the Whatstheirnames were any more alive as a result of this exchange. Just the opposite, in fact.

And for my brother and sister, speaking often came down to the following:

"Where's my box of LEGOs?"

"Don't know."

"Liar! You took it!"

"Did not."

"Tell me where it is!"

And then they hit each other. Talking was a prelude to fighting.

When dear, sweet Nishio-san spoke to me, it was most often to tell me, with that laugh the Japanese reserve for truly horrific matters, how her sister had been run over by the Kobe-to-Nishinomiya train when a child. Every time Nishio-san told me this story, she killed the poor little girl all over again. Talking was useful for killing someone.

Careful examination of what other people said led me to the conclusion that speaking was as much a creative as a destructive act. I decided I would need to be careful about what to do with this discovery.

I had also noted that words could be harmless. "Nice weather, isn't it?" or "Sweetie, don't you look terrific!" were phrases with absolutely zero impact. You could utter them without fear. You could even not utter them at all. When someone used them it was probably to alert someone else that they were not going to kill him. It was like my brother's squirt gun. When he shot it at me and said, "Bang! You're dead!" I didn't die; I only got wet. He said this kind of thing to show me he was shooting blanks.

My sixth word was "death."

THE HOUSE SEEMED ABNORMALLY QUIET. I went downstairs to find out what was going on. My father was in the living room, crying. This was an unimaginable sight, and one that was never to be repeated. My mother held him in her arms as if he were a child.

She told me very softly, "Your papa has lost his mama. Your grandmother is dead."

I looked like I was going to throw a tantrum.

My mother continued. "I know you don't know what 'death' means. You're only two and a half."

"Death!" I said in an assertive tone, then turned around and left the room.

Death! As if I didn't know! As if my two and a half years were behind me, when actually their effects stretched out before me. Death! Who knew better than I did what it meant? I had just escaped it. I knew more about it than the other children. I had extended non-life out beyond human limits. Had I not just spent two years living in a coma (for all that it can be said that one lives in a coma)? What had they thought I was doing in my crib all that time, if not killing life, killing time, killing fear, killing nothing?

Death was something I had examined carefully. Death was the ceiling. When you knew the ceiling better than you knew yourself, that was death. The ceiling was what kept your eyes from seeing higher and your thoughts from rising. When you said "ceiling" you mean "tomb." The ceiling was the top of the skull. When death came, a giant lid was lowered onto your brainpan. Something uncommon had happened to me: I had lived it in the other direction, at an age when my memory, if it could not retain death, could at least preserve its faint impression.

When the subway comes out of the tunnel, when the black curtains are thrown open, when asphyxia stops, when the only eyes we need to see us look at us anew, the lid of death lifts, and the tomb of our brain stands opens to the endless sky.

Those who have known death from close up and survived turn into Eurydices: they know that something in them recalls death too clearly and that it is best not to look at it in the face. Like a terrier, like a room with closed curtains, like solitude, death is both horrible and seductive. We feel we might be happy there. All we have to do is let ourselves fall into hibernation. So compelling is Eurydice that sometimes we forget why we should resist her.

But we must resist, if only for the reason that our voyage is one way. And if it isn't, we don't need to resist at all.

⁂

I SAT ON THE STAIRS, thinking about my grandmother and her white chocolate. She had helped liberate me from death, and soon after it was her turn. I felt there had been some kind of exchange. She had paid for my life with hers. Had she known that?

My memory would keep her alive. My grandmother had given me memory. A fair return. She is still alive, carrying her bar of white chocolate like a queen her scepter. This is my way of giving her back what she gave me.

I didn't cry. I went back to my room and played with that most wonderful of all things, the top. I made it spin round and round, watching with fascination, hour after hour. Perpetual motion lent me a look of gravity.

⁂

YES, I UNDERSTOOD what death was. But understanding wasn't enough. I had so many questions to ask. The problem was that, officially, I was limited to the use of six words and not one of them so far as I knew was a verb. How hard it was to ask a question without a verb. In my head, of course, I had all the words I needed, but how was I to go from being thought capable of uttering six words to uttering a thousand—just like that—without revealing my secret?

My solution was my nanny, Nishio-san. She spoke, as I've said, only Japanese, and this limited her exchanges with my mother. I could conceal myself behind her language.

"Nishio-san, why do we die?"

"You can talk!"

"Yes, but don't tell anyone. It's a secret."

"But your parents would be pleased to know you can talk!"

"I want to surprise them. Why do we die?"

"Because God wills it."

"Do you believe that?"

"I don't know. I have seen many people die. My sister was hit by a train. My parents and brothers were killed by bombs during the war. I don't know whether or not God wanted them to die."

"So why do we die?"

"Are you thinking about your grandmother? Dying when you're old is normal."

"Why?"

"When one has lived a long life, one is tired. For an old person, dying is like going to sleep. It is a good thing."

"What about dying young?"

"I don't know why that happens. . . . Do you really understand everything I'm saying to you?"

"Yes."

"You learned how to speak Japanese before you learned to speak French?"

"They're the same thing."

And indeed, I hadn't known there were such things as separate languages, only that there was one great big language and that one could choose either the Japanese version of it or the French version, whichever you preferred. I had not yet heard a language I couldn't understand.

"If it's the same thing, why can't I speak French?"

"I don't know. Tell me about the bombs."

"Are you sure you want to know?"

"Yes."

Nishio-san began to speak of the nightmare. One morning in 1945, when she was seven, bombs started to rain down on Kobe. She had heard them before, but only far off in the distance. That morning, Nishio-san knew that these bombs were for intended for her family, and she was right. She was lying on the *tatami,* hoping that death would come to her while she was asleep. Suddenly there was an enormous explosion right next to her, and she felt ripped into tiny pieces. Surprised to discover that she was alive, she tried to move, to find out whether her limbs were still attached to her body, but something prevented her. It took her a while to realize that she had been buried alive.

She started to dig with her hands, hoping she was digging upward, though not certain this was so. Then she came across something in the dirt—an arm. She didn't know whether or not it was still attached to a body, but she knew for certain that its owner was dead.

Suddenly she thought she might be digging in the wrong direction. She stopped and listened. *I must head toward the noise. That is where there is life.* She had heard cries and started to dig in their direction.

"How did you breathe?" I asked.

"I don't know. Somehow I did. There are animals that live in the earth, and they manage. There was little air, but there was some. Do you want to know what happened next?"

I replied enthusiastically that I did.

Finally, Nishio-san came to the surface. *That is where there is life* remained her guiding instinct. It had misled her. That was where there was death. Among the skeletons of the houses were shreds of human flesh. She had barely enough time to recognize her father's head when there was another great explosion, and she was again buried by debris.

At first she wondered whether she shouldn't stay there, sheltered in her earth tomb. *At least there's more security here, and fewer horrors.* Then, little by little, she started to suffocate. She dug toward the noise, terrified of what she would find this time. She needn't have worried. The moment she emerged she was buried again.

"I don't know how long it lasted. I dug and I dug, and each time I made it to the surface I was buried by another explosion. I don't know why I crawled upward and yet I did, again and again, because the instinct was stronger than I was. I knew that my father was dead and that my house was gone. I didn't know what had happened to my mother and my brothers. When the bombing finally stopped, I was so surprised that I was still alive. Clearing away debris, we came upon the bodies, whole or in pieces, of those missing. My mother and my brothers were among them. I was jealous of my sister, who had been hit by a train two years earlier, because she had escaped this nightmare."

Nishio-san told such wonderful stories. They always ended with body parts.

BECAUSE I WAS BECOMING SO DEMANDING of Nishio-san, my parents decided to hire a second Japanese nanny to help her. They placed an announcement in the village.

Only one person applied for the job.

Thus Kashima-san became my second nanny. Kashima-san was the opposite of Nishio-san, who was young and gentle and sweet. Nishio-san was not pretty and came from poverty. Kashima-san was around fifty and her beauty was as aristocratic as her background. She belonged to that ancient Japanese nobility the Americans abolished in 1945. For nearly thirty years, she had been a princess, and then one day she found herself without a title and without money.

Since then, she had survived by doing various tasks, such as the one my parents hired her to do. She blamed all white people for her poverty and hated every one of us, without exception. Her perfect manners and elegant aspect inspired respect. My parents spoke to her with all the deference due a very great lady; she did not speak to them in return, and did the least amount of work possible. When my mother asked her to help with some task, Kashima-san sighed and gave her a look that signified, "Whom do you take me for?"

Kashima-san treated Nishio-san like a dog, not only because the younger woman came from a humble background, but also because Kashima-san thought she was a traitor who was trafficking with the enemy. She let Nishio-san do all the work. The latter felt a misguided but unswerving sense of obedience toward the older woman, who insulted her at the slightest cause.

"Can't you hear how you speak to them?"

"I speak to them the way they speak to me."

"You lack any sense of honor. Is it not enough how they humiliated us in nineteen forty-five?"

"It was not them."

"They are all the same. These people were allies of the Americans."

"They were young children during the war. Like I was."

"So what? Their parents were our enemies. Leopards don't change their spots. I despise them all."

"You must not say such things in front of the child," said Nishio-san, indicating me.

"This baby?"

"She understands what you're saying."

"So much the better."

"I love her."

She was speaking the truth. Nishio-san loved me as much as she loved her own daughters, ten-year-old identical twins whom she never called by their first names, because she couldn't tell one from the other. She always called them *futago,* and for a long time I believed that this was the name of just one child (indications of plurality in Japanese are often very vague). One day the girls came to our house and Nishio-san called to them from afar. *Futago!* They came running like Siamese cats, thus revealing to me the meaning of the word. Being a twin must be a more serious problem in Japan than elsewhere.

I soon discovered that my age entitled me to special status. In the land of the Rising Sun, a child is a god from birth to the age he goes to nursery school. Nishio-san treated me like a divinity. My brother, my sister, and the *futago* had left behind this sacred stage of life. One therefore spoke to them in an ordinary way. But I was an *okosama*: a most honorable and excellent child, a lord child.

When I came down to the kitchen in the morning, Nishio-san bent over to my height. She gave me everything I asked for. If I wanted to eat from her plate, she let me take as much as I pleased, waiting until I had finished before eating anything herself (if by some great act of generosity I had left her anything at all).

One day at lunchtime my mother saw me do this and scolded me sharply. She pleaded with Nishio-san not to let herself be tyrannized in this way. My mother's efforts were doomed. The minute her back was turned I went back to what I was doing. I had good reason for this, for Nishio-san's *okonomiyaki* (cabbage pancake with shrimp and ginger) and *tsuke-mono* rice (rice with horseradish soaked in yellow saffron brinc) were infinitely more appealing than pureed carrots with small bits of meat.

There were two meals: one in the dining room and one in the kitchen. I nibbled during the first to leave room for the second. Very soon I had taken sides: choosing between my parents, who treated me like the others, and my nanny, who treated me like a god, was not a real choice.

I would become Japanese.

AND SO, AT THE AGE OF TWO and a half, in the province of Kansai, in the village of Shukugawa, I became Japanese.

To be Japanese meant living among beauty and adoration. To be Japanese meant inhaling the intoxicating odor of flowers in a garden moistened from rain; sitting on the edge of a pool, gazing at distant mountains as large as the heart they contained; and feeling rapture at the mystical song of the yam seller who passed through the neighborhood at twilight.

Most of all, to be Japanese meant being Nishiosan's chosen one. If I asked her, she would drop whatever she was doing, coddle me in her arms, and sing to me about gardens and blossoming cherry trees.

She was always ready to tell me those stories about bodies getting cut to pieces, at which I marveled, or about the witch who cooked people in a soup cauldron. I listened to these delightful tales in stunned silence.

Nishio-san sat and cradled me like a doll. I sometimes pretended to be hurt so that she would comfort me. She played along, consoling me endlessly for my nonexistent suffering, gazing at me with consuming piteousness.

Then her delicate finger would trace my features and exalt my extreme beauty. She exulted in my mouth, forehead, cheeks. Never, she said, had she seen so beautiful a face as mine. Nishio-san was a good person.

And I never tired of being held in her arms. I would always stay there, bathed in her idolatry, proof of the rightness and excellence of my divine self.

At the age of two and a half, I would have been an idiot not to be Japanese.

Not by accident had I revealed my knowledge of Japanese first. The cult of myself involved linguistic requirements. I needed an idiom in which to communicate with my followers. These were not numerous, my followers, but because of the intensity of their reverence and the importance of their place in my universe they would do: Nishio-san, the *futago,* and passersby.

When I walked in the street, holding the hand of the high priestess of my adoration, I awaited with great serenity the acclamation of my servants. I could be sure they would always sing my praises.

Nonetheless, the practice of this religion was never more pleasing than within the four walls of the garden, my temple. A small yard with planted flowers and trees and surrounded by a wall—nothing better than a garden has ever been invented to reconcile humanity and universe.

It was a Japanese garden, which is a redundancy. It was Zen but its stone pool, its utter simplicity, and its variety of plants and trees spoke of the country that, more religiously than any other, has defined what a garden should be.

Belief in me achieved its greatest degree of intensity in the garden. The high walls, capped with tiles, protected me from the prying eyes of the laity. Here was my sanctuary.

When God required a place to symbolize earthly delights, He didn't choose a desert island, or a beach with fine sand, or a field of ripened wheat, or a lush hillside; He chose a garden.

I shared His preference, for there is no better place on earth from which to reign. In my garden fiefdom, plants were my subjects. At my command they would blossom before my eyes. This was the first Spring of my existence and I couldn't yet imagine that this vegetal refulgence would reach a high-point, and then decline.

One evening, I said to a stalk on which there was a bud, "blossom." And the next day it became a glorious white peony. I had powers—of that there wasn't any doubt. When I spoke of them to Nishio-san she didn't try to deny that this was so.

Beginning with the birth of my memory, that February, the world had not ceased from offering up its glories to me. Nature was allied to my progress. Every day the garden was more luxuriant than it was the day before. One flower would fade only to be reborn in more stunning fashion a step or two away.

And how grateful everyone was for what I had done. How drab their lives had been before me! I had brought them a profusion of marvels. What could make their adoration more apt?

＊　＊　＊

THERE WAS ONE HITCH IN ALL THIS. Kashima-san, of course.

Kashima-san didn't believe in me. She was the only Japanese woman who did not accept this new religion. She hated me. Grammarians are naïve enough to believe that the exception proves the rule; I didn't, and Kashima-san's impiety seriously vexed me.

She wouldn't let me eat from her plate. Stunned by

this impertinence, I tried to eat from it nonetheless. She slapped me.

Sick from outrage, I found Nishio-san and told her what had happened, hoping she would punish Kashima-san for this sacrilege.

"Do you find this normal?" I asked indignantly.

"It is Kashima-san. That is how she is."

I wondered whether that was an acceptable response. Did anyone have the right to slap me for the sole reason that "that was how she was?" I deemed it was not acceptable. Anyone who dared question my religion would have to pay.

I commanded Kashima-san's garden not to blossom. This had no effect that I could perceive. Perhaps she did not like flowers. Then I was told that she did not have a garden.

That being the case, I decided upon a more charitable approach, and set out to charm her utterly. I stood in front of her with a magnanimous smile and extended my hand, the way God does to Adam on the ceiling of the Sistine Chapel. She ignored it.

Kashima-san refused me; she denied me. She was the equivalent of the anti-Christ; she was the anti-me.

I felt deep sorrow for her. How terrible it must have been for her not to adore me. Nishio-san and my other loyal followers radiated happiness, because it did them so much good to love me.

Kashima-san did not avail herself of this sweetness and light—you could read it in her hard, handsome features, in her pinched expression and air of disdain. I circled around her, observing her, seeking out the reason for her lack of interest in me. I never imagined that it could have anything to do with me, of course; that I was divine was beyond question. If my aristocratic nanny didn't love me, it was because *she* had a problem.

I found out what it was. Having studied Kashima-san carefully, I could see that she suffered from the disease of self-denial. Every time there was cause for rejoicing or celebration, the mouth of this noble lady would tighten and her lips become set. She always held back. It was as if such pleasures were beneath her, as if joy were an abdication.

I undertook several scientific experiments. I brought to Kashima-san the most fragrant camellia from the garden, informing her that I had picked it especially for her. Her mouth tightened; she thanked me curtly. I asked Nishio-san to make Kashima-san her favorite dish. Nishio-san prepared a sublime *chawan mushi,* which Kashima-san nibbled at delicately and in complete silence. When I saw a rainbow, I ran to Kashima-san so that we could admire it together; she shrugged her shoulders.

In my infinite generosity, and as a last resort, I decided to present Kashima-san with the most beautiful sight imaginable. I dressed up in a traditional Japanese outfit Nishio-san had given me: a little red silk kimono decorated with water lilies, a large red *obi,* lacquered *geta,* and a parasol made of purple paper on which was an image of storks in flight. I applied some of my mother's red lipstick and went to look at myself in the mirror. I was, without the slightest doubt, magnificent. Who could resist such a vision?

First, I allowed myself to be admired by my most loyal followers, who cried out in ecstasy. Spinning and fluttering like a butterfly, I danced around the garden, then picked an enormous peony and perched it on my head.

I presented myself to Kashima-san. She offered no reaction.

This confirmed my suspicion: she suffered from self-denial. She was holding back. How else could she have exhibited such indifference at the sight of me? Like God before a sinner, I felt keen sorrow for her. Poor, poor Kashima-san!

Had I known that there was such a thing, I would have offered up a prayer for her. I saw no way of integrating this sad creature into my vision of the world. I mourned this deeply.

I had also discovered the limits of my power.

AMONG MY FATHER'S FRIENDS was a Vietnamese businessman who had married a French woman. Because of political turmoil of the sort easily imaginable in Vietnam in 1970, the man suddenly had to return home, taking with him his wife but leaving behind their six-year-old son Hugo, who was placed in my parents' care for an indeterminate amount of time.

Hugo was a serious and reserved boy. He had made a good impression on me until the moment he went over to the enemy—my brother. The two boys became inseparable. To punish him, I decided not to name Hugo.

I had as yet spoken only a few words in French. This was becoming unbearable. I experienced a crippling need to express such crucial perceptions as

56

"Hugo and André are made of green caca," but I was not thought capable of such sophisticated assertions. This frustrated me, knowing that the boys were losing nothing by waiting for me to express their true nature.

Sometimes I wondered why I didn't simply reveal the full extent of my speaking abilities. What was the point of holding back? Without knowing it, I was adhering strictly to the etymology of the word "infant"—"incapable of speech"—and somehow thought, confusedly, that by speaking I would have lost some of the respect due to prophets and to the mentally impaired.

In southern Japan April is a month of refulgent sweetness. My parents took all of us to the seashore. I already knew what the sea was, having become a little familiar with Osaka Bay, which, at the time, was a cesspool. Swimming in it was out of the question. So we crossed to the other side of the country, to Tottori, where I first discovered the Sea of Japan and was captivated by it. The Japanese consider the sea to be male, whereas they deem the ocean to be female. The logic of this distinction escaped me. It still escapes me.

The beach at Tottori was as wide as a desert. Crossing it seemed to take forever. When I finally reached the water, it turned out to be as afraid of me as I was of it. Like a timid child, it approached and then ran away. I did the same.

Everybody else dove in. My mother called me to follow but I didn't dare, despite the inflatable plastic tube around my waist. I looked at the sea with terror and desire. Mama took me by the hand and led me in.

The fluid took me and bounced me on its surface. Suddenly I had escaped the pull of the earth. I screamed in ecstasy. As majestic as a miniature Saturn and its ring, I stayed in the water for hours on end, and would only be dragged out by force.

"Sea!"

My seventh word.

*　*　*

I QUICKLY LEARNED to do without the tube, having discovered that by working my arms and legs I could manage to swim as well as any other idiot. Because doing this was so tiring, however, I always stayed where I could touch bottom.

Something wonderful happened one day. I went out into the sea and began to walk straight ahead, toward Korea, and found that the water wasn't getting any deeper. I had mysteriously caused the sea floor to rise up. To each her own miracles. I decided that I would proceed all the way to the Asian continent.

I launched out into the unknown, my feet caressing the sandy bottom. I walked and walked, taking giant steps away from Japan, thinking how wonderful it was that I had such fabulous powers.

Then I fell. The seabed that had borne me aloft had fallen away and I lost my footing. The water swallowed me. I kicked and clawed my way to the surface, but each time I got my head above water a wave pushed me back down, like a torturer intent on extracting a confession.

I knew that I was drowning. When my head was above water I could see the beach, which looked very far away, and my parents, who were napping. I could also see that people were watching me drown. They did nothing to stop it. They were adhering to the ancient Japanese principle of never saving another's life, because doing so creates a crushing debt of gratitude.

The public spectacle of my dying was even more terrifying than actually dying.

"Tasukete!" I yelled.

The people just stared.

My reticence about speaking French now seemed totally absurd. *"Au secours!"* I screamed.

It suddenly dawned on me that perhaps that was what the water had wanted: get me to admit that I spoke the language of my parents. The problem was they couldn't hear me. And so committed were the Japanese onlookers to their principle of nonintervention that it even extended to not alerting my parents. Everyone was watching me drown with close attention.

Soon I was too tired to kick, and let myself sink, my body sliding beneath the waves. These were the final moments of my life and I didn't want to miss them, so I managed to open my eyes. What I saw was truly marvelous. The sunlight had never seemed as dazzling as it did from under the water. The movement of the waves produced silent clouds of sparkles.

I was so mesmerized by the sight that I forgot to be afraid. It felt as if I had been there for hours.

Then arms were grabbing me and hauling me up toward the light. I took a deep, gasping breath. My mother was crying. She ran back to the beach, holding me tight against her.

She wrapped me in a towel and massaged my back and chest vigorously. I threw up lots of water. Then she cradled me and, through her tears, told me how I had been saved.

"Hugo saw you. He was playing with André and Juliette when he saw your head disappear under the water. He came to warn me and pointed to where you were. If it hadn't been for him, you'd be dead!"

I looked at Hugo and said, with great solemnity, "Thank you, Hugo. You're nice."

There followed a moment of stunned silence.

My father began to shout.

"She can talk! She can talk like an empress!"

He went from jubilation to silent, introspective shivering, then back to whoops of laughter.

"I've been talking for a long time," I replied, shrugging my shoulders.

The sea had done what it had set out to do. I had confessed.

* * *

LYING ON THE BEACH next to my sister, I wondered whether I was happy not to be dead. I looked at Hugo as if he were a mathematical equation. Without him, no me. No me. Would that have pleased me? *I would not be here to know if it pleased me or not*, I told myself logically. Yes, I was happy not to be dead, and knowing that pleased me.

Next to me was pretty Juliette. Above me, the glorious clouds. Before me, the wondrous sea. Behind me, the infinite beach. The world was beautiful. Living was worth the effort.

* * *

WHEN WE GOT BACK TO SHUKUGAWA I decided to learn to swim. Not far from our house in the mountains was a little green lake that I had baptized Little Green Lake. It was a small paradise. The water was warm and velvety, the shores fringed by azalea bushes.

Every morning, Nishio-san took me to this lake. All by myself I learned how to swim underwater like a fish, my eyes open to the marvels whose existence drowning had shown me.

When my head came up, I could see the tree-covered mountains rising up around me. I was at the geometric center of an ever-widening circle of splendor.

■ ■ ■

MY BRUSH WITH DEATH had not shaken my unarticulated conviction that I was divine. After all, why would the gods be immortal? What did immortality have to do with divinity? Was a peony any less sublime simply because eventually it would wilt?

I asked Nishio-san who Jesus was. She told me she didn't really know.

"I know that he's a god," she offered. "And that he has long hair."

"Do you believe in him?"

"No."

"Do you believe in me?"

"Yes."

"I have long hair."

"Yes. Besides, I know you."

Nishio-san was a good person. She always had good reasons for things.

My brother, my sister, and Hugo went to the

American school near Mount Rokko. Among André's schoolbooks was one entitled *My Friend Jesus*. I couldn't read it, but I looked at the pictures. Toward the end of the book there was one of Jesus, hanging on the cross, with lots of people watching him. The picture fascinated me. I asked Hugo why Jesus was on a cross.

"To kill him," he replied.

"Being put on a cross kills people?"

"Yes, because they nailed him to it. The nails are what kill you."

This explanation seemed acceptable, and it made the picture all the more fascinating to me. Jesus was in the process of dying in front of a whole crowd of people, and no one tried to save him.

I, too, had once been dying, watching people watch me. All anyone in the picture had to do was come forward and take the nails out, just as when I was drowning all anyone would have had to have done was take me out of the water—or at least warn my parents. In both of our cases, Jesus' and mine, people had decided against getting involved.

It seemed clear the inhabitants of this crucifying country adhered to the same principles as the Japanese. Saving someone's life reduced him to a lifetime of slavery of exaggerated gratitude. Better to let someone die than to deprive him of his freedom.

Questioning this precept never occurred to me. All I knew was that it was terrible to feel yourself dying in front of people. I felt a strong bond with Jesus. I was sure I knew how he must have felt.

I wanted to know more about the story. Because the truth seemed to be locked in the rectangular pages of books, I decided to learn to read them. When I informed my family of my decision, I was laughed at.

As I wasn't taken seriously, I decided to learn to read on my own. This wouldn't pose a problem. I had learned to do equally remarkable things all by myself: walking, talking, swimming, ruling, and spinning the top.

Beginning with my brother's Tintin books made the most sense. They had pictures. I took one down at random, sat on the floor, and turned the pages. I don't think I could tell you how it happened, but by the time a cow who went into a building came out through a faucet that made sausages, I had discovered how to read. I was careful not to reveal this fact to anyone. They would have laughed at me.

April is the month when the cherry trees bloom. The neighborhood celebrated this in the evening by drinking sake. Nishio-san gave me a glass. I howled with delight.

I SPENT MY NIGHTS standing on my pillow, gripping the bars of my crib, staring at my father and mother as if preparing notes for a behavioral study about them. They felt a growing unease about this. The steadiness of my gaze intimidated them to the point that they started to lose sleep. It was time I slept somewhere other than in their room.

I was moved into a kind of attic, which thrilled me. Here was a whole new ceiling to look at, and from a first glance the cracks seemed more expressive than those on the ceiling in my parents' bedroom, the ones I had been observing for the previous two and a half years. There were also piles of objects to subject to my avid visual interrogation: trunks, old clothes, a deflated kiddy pool, beaten-up tennis racquets, and boxes.

Soon I was staring at the boxes, thinking that whatever they contained must be very precious. The crib was much too high for me to climb out and investigate for myself, much as I wanted to.

At the end of April, a wonderful new thing happened: the window in my room was left open at night. I didn't think I had ever slept with an open window, and what an incredible thing it turned out to be. I could register all those strange sounds that those who sleep remain ignorant of, interpreting what they meant, endowing them with meaning. My crib was placed directly below the window, and when the night breeze blew the curtains open I saw the violet sky. It was comforting to learn that night was not jet black.

My favorite noise was the distant barking of some unidentifiable and tormented dog, which I baptized *Yorukoé*—"evening voice." His howling irritated the entire neighborhood, but I thought it possessed a melancholy beauty. I wanted to know why the animal was in such pain.

The sweet night air flowed through the window and straight into my bed. I drank it in and became intoxicated. I would have loved the universe for nothing else than for this alone.

My hearing and sense of smell worked full time during these endless April nights. The desire to look out the screenless window was almost overpowering.

The window was like a porthole in the dark hold of a ship. It drew me irresistibly.

One night I couldn't bear it any longer. Climbing to the top of the bars, I stretched my arms as far as they would go and found that my hands could just touch the sill. Drunk with success, I managed to haul myself up and perch my upper body on the window ledge.

I peered out into the nocturnal landscape, gazing wonderingly at the dark silhouettes of the mountains, the majestic roofs of the neighboring houses, the phosphorescence of the cherry trees in bloom, the mystery of the dark streets.

I wanted to lean out farther, so that I could see the spot in the side yard where Nishio-san hung the laundry. When I shifted my weight, the inevitable happened. I fell.

Instinctively spreading my legs, somehow I managed to hook my feet on the inside of the window frame, wedging my calves and thighs against the edge of the roof and my hips against the gutter. My head and upper body dangled over the void.

Once the first terror had passed, I found this position afforded me a new observation post. I looked with enormous interest at the back of the house. I also found that I could sway back and forth, and make my spit perform balletic exercises.

When my mother came into my room the next morning she cried out in horror. Above the empty crib were the window with the curtains pushed open and my feet on either side. She grabbed me by my ankles, hauled me inside, and gave me the spanking of the century.

* * *

IT WAS DECIDED that the attic would become my brother's room, and that I would take his place in Juliette's room. This began another new life for me. We would share a room for the next fifteen years.

Now I spent my long nights observing my sister. The fairies that had visited her in infancy had blessed her with the ability to sleep deeply and gracefully; in fact they had made her graceful in every way possible. She wasn't in the least bothered by my staring. I learned by heart the rhythm of her breathing and the music of her sighs. No one knew so well the sleep of another.

Twenty years later, I read a poem by Louis Aragon and felt a shiver of recognition:

I returned home in stealth as do prowlers
You were already in the heavy sleep of flowers [. . .]
I'm afraid of your silence, yet you breathe still
Against me, holding you, imagination fills
Next to you, I am the watcher who is troubled

With each step he takes he hears its echo doubled
In deepest night
Next to you, I am the watcher from the walls
Who winces when one leaf dies and falls
       Murmuring
In deepest night
I live for this plaintive song at your hour of repose
I live for this fear of all things closed
In deepest night
O my gazelle, tell those who inhabit the future
That here the name Elsa alone is my signature
In deepest night.

    All I had to do was replace "Elsa" with "Juliette."

    She slept for us both. In the morning I woke up, refreshed by my sister's sleep.

MAY STARTED OFF WELL.

The azalea bushes around Little Green Lake began to bloom gloriously. It was as if a spark had set off an explosion; the color spread across the entire mountain. The place where I swam was surrounded in brilliant pink.

I was on the point of believing May a most excellent month when a crisis erupted. In the garden, for reasons that escaped me, my parents hoisted up, like a flag, a giant fish made of red paper, which clattered in the wind.

I asked what it was for, this red fish, and was told it was a carp, and that it was customary to raise one up in May, because it was the month of boys. I didn't see the connection, I replied. I was told that the carp was the symbol of boys and that one raised it in the homes of families hoping to have a baby boy.

"Which is the month of girls?" I inquired.

"There isn't one."

This dumbfounded me. What sort of staggering injustice was this?

My brother and Hugo gave me a teasing look.

"Why does a carp stand for a boy?" I asked again.

"Why do children always ask why?" was the only reply I got.

Deeply irritated, I left the garden, still sure that my question had been highly pertinent.

I had, of course, already noticed the difference between boys and girls, but this had never particularly concerned me. There were lots of differences here on earth—between the Japanese and the Belgians (I assumed all white people were Belgians, except myself, of course; I was Japanese); little people and tall people; nice people and nasty people; Nishio-san and Kashima-san; and so on. It seemed to me that the male and female opposition was but one of many. For the first time, I suspected there was more to it.

I sat beneath the pole and observed the paper carp. Why did it express my brother's identity more than mine? And why was masculinity so terrific that it deserved its own month—not just any month, but the month of sweet air and blooming azaleas—while femininity didn't get so much as a pennant, or even its own day?

I kicked the pole. Perhaps May wasn't so great. The cherry trees had lost their flowers—it had been a kind of fall in spring. Freshness had begun to fade.

Perhaps it was right that May be the month of boys. It was when things started to decline.

*   *   *

I DEMANDED TO BE SHOWN some real carp, the way an emperor might demand of his subjects that they show him a real elephant.

Nothing is easier than finding carp in Japan, particularly during May. In fact, you can't get away from them. In any public garden, as soon as there is any water, there are carp. These *koi* are not intended to be eaten—carp *sashimi* would be revolting—but to be observed and admired. Going to a park to see them is considered an activity as civilized as going to a concert.

Nishio-san took me to the famous Futatabi Arboretum. I strolled with my nose in the air, awed by the splendor of the unbelievably immense and ancient cryptomeria. I was two and three-quarters; these trees were two hundred and fifty years old. That meant they were nearly a hundred times older.

Futatabi is a plant sanctuary, and even if, as I did,

you lived in the heart of Japan's most beautiful countryside, you couldn't help being captivated by the magnificence of its garden arrangements. The trees there seem aware of their special status.

We came to a pond. I could see a tumbling of color. On the other side of the pond a priest had just strewn some crumbs on the water, and the carp were rushing to catch them. Some of them were huge. They left an iridescent trail of color, ranging from steel blue to orange, and including white, black, silver, and gold.

If you squinted, all you could see were bright sparks of light, and think how marvelous this was. But opening your eyes forced upon you the loathsome sight of these corpulent aquatic divas, these farcically over-stuffed aristocrats of the fish world.

Lying on the bottom, they looked like mute Lady Castafiores—the fat lady in the Tintin comic books, the one always singing loudly off key. Their motley colors made them seem like plump, fur-coated sausages, or like great chunks of ghostly white bacon fat with bright tattoos. There could be nothing more repugnant than carp, I concluded. No wonder they were the symbol for boys.

"They live to be over a hundred," Nishio-san told me in a tone of great respect.

I wasn't sure that was anything to boast about. Longevity wasn't an end in and of itself. The long lives of the cryptomeria lent amplitude to their venerable nobility. Old age only emphasized their regal dominion, and earned these monuments of power and patience the reverential awe that was their due.

A hundred years for a carp meant a century of stewing in its own lard, watching its moist, fetid fishy flesh grow saturated with stagnant water. Only one thing is more revolting than young fat—old fat.

I kept these opinions to myself. We returned to the house. Nishio-san assured everyone that I had loved the carp. I didn't deny this, too wearied by the thought of explaining my views.

*   *   *

ANDRÉ, HUGO, JULIETTE, AND I took baths together. The gangly, knobby-kneed boys looked nothing like carp. That didn't prevent them from being ugly. Maybe that was it, I thought—the basis of this boy-*koi* connection: being gross. Girls could never have been represented by so repugnant a creature.

I asked my mother to take me to the "apuarium" (I was strangely unable to pronounce the word "aquarium") in Kobe, one of the finest in the world. My parents were surprised by my sudden passion for fish.

I only wanted to see how other fish compared to carp. I spent a long time standing in front of the glass tanks, and each creature I gazed at seemed more admirable than the one before. Some were as phantas-magoric as abstract art. They were so ungainly and yet so graceful.

My conclusion was categorical: of all fish, the one at the very bottom—the *only* one at the bottom—was the carp. I snickered. My mother noticed this and was delighted. *My little girl will be a marine biologist,* she thought.

The Japanese were absolutely right. The carp was the ideal symbol for boys.

I loved my father, I put up with Hugo—he had saved my life, after all—but my brother was the worst nuisance imaginable. His sole ambition in life seemed to be to torment me; he took infinite pleasure in it. When he had succeeded in enraging me for hours on end, his day was complete. I wondered whether all older brothers were this way. Perhaps, I thought, they should be exterminated.

WITH JUNE CAME THE HEAT. I started living in the garden, never leaving it except when I was forced to go up to bed. The fish flag had been lowered on the first day of the month; the season of honoring boys had ended. It was as if someone had toppled the statue of an oppressor. No more carp marred the view. June promised to be a good month.

The temperature meant outdoor performances. I was told that we were going to hear my father sing.

"Papa sings?"

"He chants Noh."

"What's that?"

"You'll see."

I had never heard my father sing.

Twenty years later, I learned why my father, about whom nothing had predisposed to a musical career, had become a Noh singer. In 1967, he had left Belgium for Osaka to serve as consul. This was his first posting in Asia and the young diplomat had instantly fallen in love with the country. Japan became, and has remained, the love of his life.

With all the enthusiasm of a neophyte, he wanted to discover every single one of its wonders. As he didn't yet speak the language, an interpreter accompanied him wherever he went, acting both as translator and as guide to all manner of Japanese culture. Given that he was so enthusiastic about Japan, she got the idea of introducing him to the least accessible and yet most revered of all traditional arts: Noh. At the time, Westerners were as closed to it as they were fond of kabuki.

She therefore took him to the famous school of Noh in Kansai, where the master teacher was considered a Living Treasure, to see a performance. My father said he felt he had stepped back a thousand years in time. This feeling became more acute when he heard the singing, which, at first, sounded like prehistoric rumblings. He experienced the sort of nervous hilarity you feel when you look at panoramas of historical scenes in museums.

But as the performance went on, he began to appreciate that what he was hearing was the very opposite of primitive; nothing could be more sophisticated and civilized. Still, to go from that to finding Noh beautiful was a step he had not yet made.

Despite the eerie, unnerving sounds, he maintained a rapt and serious expression on his face. The threnody went on for many hours, but he managed to keep his boredom from being apparent.

Merely my father's presence at the school had created a stir. After the performance was over, the Living Treasure himself approached my father and said,

"Honorable guest, this is the first time an outsider has entered this place. Might I ask your opinion of what you have heard?"

He had spoken in Japanese, of course. The interpreter did her job.

Not knowing what to say, my father offered a few harmless clichés about the importance of ancestral traditions, the richness of the artistic heritage in this country, and other touching inanities.

The interpreter, an educated and refined woman, was horrified by such banalities, and decided not to translate so inadequate a response. She formulated her own elegant opinion and exchanged it for my father's.

While she was "translating" my father's reply, the venerable old master's eyes grew wide. How was it possible that an uninitiated white, who had only recently arrived in Japan and just heard Noh for the first time in his life, had already grasped the essence and subtlety of this supreme art?

In an extraordinary gesture for a Japanese—especially a Living Treasure—he took this foreigner's hand and said with great solemnity,

"Honored guest, you are a prodigy! An exceptional being! You must become one of my students!"

And because my father, though young, was already an accomplished diplomat, he immediately replied,

"Nothing would give me greater pleasure."

He didn't have a clue such politeness would have any consequences, and assumed that any arrangement would soon be forgotten. Then the venerable old master instructed him to come to his first lesson the day after tomorrow, at seven.

Any sane man would have known the simplest thing to do was have his secretary call the next day and simply cancel the appointment by phone. Instead, my honorable father got up at dawn on the day in question and arrived on time for his lesson. The venerable old master seemed not at all surprised and launched straight into the lesson, making no concessions whatever to my father's linguistic weaknesses, believing that so great a spirit as this had earned the honor of being taken seriously.

By the end of the lesson my poor father was exhausted.

"Very good," said the master. "Come tomorrow at the same hour."

"Ah, well you see . . . the problem is that I have to be at work at eight-thirty," he said through the interpreter, who had, of course, accompanied him to the lesson.

"That is not a problem. You will come at five in the morning."

His new student meekly consented. From that day on, my father went to the school every morning at this ungodly hour, inhuman for someone with such a demanding day job, except on weekends, when he was permitted to take his lesson at the very leisurely hour of seven.

The truth was my honorable father felt crushed by the immensity of what he was trying to absorb. The man who had arrived in Japan loving football and cycling wondered by what bizarre sequence of events he found himself sacrificing his life at the altar of so abstruse an art. It seemed to him that Noh matched him about as well as Jansenism would a bon vivant or asceticism a slob.

He was wrong, however, and the venerable old master turned out to be right. He had uncovered within the capacious chest of this blue-eyed foreigner a Noh-producing organ of the first order.

"You are a remarkable singer," he later told my

father, who in the meantime had learned to speak Japanese. "I am therefore going to complete your education by teaching you to dance."

"To . . . dance! But, Venerable Master, look at me," stammered my father, displaying his expansive girth.

"I do not see where the problem lies. We will start the dance lesson tomorrow morning at five."

The next day, at the end of the class, it was the teacher's turn to be unnerved. In the course of three hours, despite his forbearance, he had not succeeded in making my father produce the slightest movement that approximated grace.

Polite but also saddened by this most unfortunate outcome, the Living Treasure said to him,

"We will make an exception in your case. You will be the singer of Noh who does not dance."

Later, between seizures of mirth, the venerable old master regaled his fellow chanters with descriptions of what a chubby Westerner looked like learning to dance with a fan.

My poor father nonetheless became an artist if not of star quality then at least of some accomplishment. He became famous throughout Japan for the name by which he is called still: "The Singer of Noh with Blue Eyes."

Every day, during the five years he worked at the

consulate in Osaka, he took his three-hour course with the venerable old master. Between them grew the powerful bond of friendship and respect that unites the disciple and his *sensei*.

■ ■ ■

WHEN I WAS TWO, of course, I knew nothing of all this. I also had no idea what my father did during the day. He came home in the evening. From where I hadn't the slightest clue.

"What does Papa do?" I asked my mother.

"He is the consul."

Here was another word that I didn't know, but whose meaning I was determined to locate.

Then came the afternoon for the performance. My mother took Hugo and the three of us to the temple. The ritual scenery of Noh had been set up outside, in the sanctuary's garden.

Like the other spectators, we were each given a hard cushion on which to kneel. It was a very beautiful spot, I thought, but I wondered what on earth was going to happen here.

The performance began. My father entered at a deliberate pace. He was wearing a wonderful Japanese costume. I felt a surge of pride.

Then he began to sing. I stifled a cry of horror. The

most awful sounds came out of his stomach. His familiar voice been transformed into an unrecognizable howl. Had something happened to him? What was he trying to say? I wanted to cry, just as you would if you had just witnessed an accident.

My mother had told me my father would be singing. When Nishio-san sang nursery rhymes, that was nice. The sounds emanating from my father's mouth were not pleasing; they scared me out of my wits. I desperately wanted to be somewhere else.

Years later I learned to like Noh, even to adore it, but for any Westerner, however well-intentioned, hearing it for the first time produces profound discomfort, the same sort of discomfort he feels when he first bites into a marinated bitter plum, the traditional Japanese breakfast staple.

It was a long afternoon. After the initial fear came tedium. The performance dragged on for four hours, during which almost nothing happened. I wondered why we were there at all. I didn't seem to be the only one to wonder this. Hugo and André were obviously bored out of their minds. Juliette had fallen fast asleep on her cushion. How I envied her for this. Even my mother struggled to stifle the occasional yawn.

My father, kneeling so as not to have to dance, delivered his interminable drone. I wondered what was going on in his head. Around me, the Japanese public listened to him impassively, a sign (as I later learned) that he was singing well.

The show finally ended at sunset. My blue-eyed father left the stage faster than tradition called for, and for good reason (as I also later learned): while the Japanese can remain kneeling for hours on end without any discomfort, the paternal limbs had apparently gone completely numb. He had sprinted to the wings before he collapsed. Luckily for him, a singer of Noh does not come back on stage to acknowledge applause, which is generally pretty sparing anyway. To applaud an artist who has just departed is considered the height of vulgarity.

That evening my father asked me what I had thought of his performance. I replied with a question.

"Is that what a consul does? Sing?"

"Not quite."

"So what does being a consul mean?"

"It's hard to explain. I'll tell you when you're older."

He's hiding something, I thought. *He must have to do pretty awful things.*

NO ONE SUSPECTED that I was reading. When I sat on the floor, a book on my lap, they thought I was looking at the pictures in a Tintin book. Actually, I was reading the Bible. The Old Testament completely escaped me, but there were some things in the New Testament that appealed to me.

For example, I liked the part where Jesus forgives Mary Magdalene. Of course I didn't understand the nature of her sins, but what was wonderful was that she got down on her knees and rubbed his feet with her long hair. I would have loved someone to do that to me.

   • • •

THE TEMPERATURE ROSE SHARPLY. July was the beginning of the rainy season. It poured nearly every day. The rain, soft and sweet, held me in its thrall.

I spent the entire day on the terrace, under the roofed portion, watching the sky attack the earth. I pretended to be the referee in these cosmic matches. I kept score. The clouds were far more impressive than the earth, but the earth always ended up winning, because it was the grand champion of the forces of inertia. When the earth saw the magnificent water-filled clouds arrive, it taunted its assailants:

Go ahead, douse me. Hit me with everything you've got. Plaster me. I won't say a word and I won't complain, for nothing can absorb like me, and when you're drained and are no more I will still be there.

Sometimes I left the shelter of the roof and lay on top of the victim to participate in the onslaught. I chose the most exciting moment, the final pounding downpour, the moment in the bout when the clouds delivered a punishing, relentless hail of blows, in a booming fracas of exploding bones.

I tried to keep my eyes open while looking up. The beauty of the storm clouds was awesome, and it saddened me to think that sooner or later they would lose. Though I was a denizen of the earth, I was rooting for the clouds. They were far more interesting, I thought, and I would have betrayed the earth for them.

Nishio-san tried to make me come out of the rain.

"You're crazy. You'll get sick."

While she removed my soaking clothes and rubbed me with a linen towel I looked at the curtain of water that continued its doomed project: to flatten the earth. It was like being in a cosmic car wash.

* * *

THE RAIN SOMETIMES WON, and when it did it was called a flood.

The water level in the neighborhood rose. This kind of thing happened every summer in the Kansai Mountains, and was not considered a catastrophe; indeed it was a yearly ritual, and in anticipation the ô-miso (the honorable storm drains) in the streets were left wide open.

When you went in a car you had to go slowly, to avoid open manholes. It was like being in a boat. There were so many reasons why the rainy season delighted me.

Little Green Lake nearly doubled its size, overflowing the azalea bushes. Sometimes there was nowhere to swim, but how wonderfully strange it was to feel a flowering bush beneath your feet in the water.

One day, taking advantage of a moment when the rains had paused, my father decided to take a walk in the neighborhood.

"Do you want to come?" he asked me, holding out his hand.

We left together to wander the flooded streets. I loved walking with my father. He would get lost in his thoughts and let me do whatever stupid things I wanted to do. My mother would never have allowed me to jump with both feet into the torrent rushing along the curbs, soaking my dress and my father's trousers in the process. He didn't seem to notice.

We lived in a true Japanese neighborhood—calm and beautiful, bordered by walls topped with tiles and overhung by ginkgoes growing in the gardens. In the distance, the street turned into a path, which wound along the mountain to Little Green Lake. Here was my universe, given especially to me, and for the only time in my life I felt a profound sense of being home. I was holding my father's hand. Everything seemed to be where it ought to be, beginning with me.

Then my hand was empty. I looked beside me. No one there. Only the moment before my father had been next to me. I had turned my head and he was gone. I hadn't even noticed when he let go of my hand.

Could someone simply disappear? Were people so fragile that you could suddenly lose them for no reason? Could someone as substantial as my father vanish? It was terrifying.

I heard his voice calling me—from beyond the tomb, I assumed, since I had looked carefully all around me and not located him. His voice seemed distant, traveling the length of the earth to reach me.

"Papa, where are you?"

"I'm here."

"Where?"

"Don't move. And don't go where I was."

"Where was that?"

"Three feet in front of you, on the right."

"What happened?"

"I fell into a drain."

I looked, but couldn't see any drain. Then I looked again and saw a whirlpool, which must signify water rushing downward.

"Are you in the *miso,* Papa?" I asked, thinking this was hilariously funny.

"Yes, sweetie," he said as calmly as possible, so as not to alarm me.

This was the wrong approach. He would have done better by alarming me. I wasn't in the least frightened now. I found the whole situation great fun, and not in the least dangerous. I looked at the whirlpool that had swallowed him, marveling that he could talk to me through this liquid wall. I wanted to join him, to see what his aquatic home was like.

"Do you like it down there, Papa?"

"Oh, it's not too bad. Go back to the house and tell Mama that I'm in the drain, okay?" He said this so matter-of-factly that I didn't sense any urgency to my mission.

"I'm going."

I turned around and headed home.

Along the way, I stopped. Something occurred to me. This was what my father did for a living! Of course! "Consul" meant "drain-keeper." He had not wanted to tell me this because he was ashamed of it. He was secretive.

I was giddy with happiness. Finally, I had uncovered the deep mystery of my father's profession. He left early in the morning and came back in the evening without my knowing where he went. Now I would know. He spent his days down in the sewers.

I was delighted that my father had a job connected with water, because although the water down there was filthy it was still water, my kinship element, the element that most resembled me, the one in which I was most at home even if I had almost drowned in it. Besides, wasn't it logical that I would have nearly died in the element that knew me best? I didn't yet know that friends are the most treacherous traitors, but I did know that the most wonderful things in life were also the most dangerous—like leaning too far out the window or lying down in the middle of the street.

These absorbing thoughts made me forget the mission my father had sent me on. I started to play on the curbs, splashing feetfirst in the cascading rivers of water and making up songs as I went. I saw a cat on a wall, afraid of getting itself wet, so I picked it up and carried it to the wall across the street, all the while informing it how fantastic swimming was and all the good things it did for you. The cat leapt away without thanking me.

I had to say that my father had chosen a strange way of showing me what he did in life. Rather than simply explaining matters, he had taken me to his workplace and then jumped into it, so that he could preserve his secret. My papa! I thought that he must also have practiced his Noh lessons in the sewers, and that was why, until that memorable first performance, I had never heard him sing.

I made a boat out of a ginkgo leaf and set it free on the current, trotting along beside it. How odd that the Japanese needed a Belgian to run their sewers! Belgians were probably the best drain-keepers in the world. It wasn't all that important. Next month was my third birthday. I wanted a stuffed toy elephant. I had made frequent allusions to it, so that my parents would get the point, but it was sometimes hard to read their reaction.

If there hadn't been all this flooding I would have played my favorite game, which I called the "Challenge." Challenge consisted of lying down in the middle of the street and singing a song and then not budging, no matter what. I always wondered whether I would have moved had a car come along. Maybe I wouldn't have! My heart beat hard at the thought. Alas, on those few occasions when I had escaped surveillance to play Challenge, not a single car had come by. I therefore could not answer my own question.

After plenty of adventures—mental, physical, subterranean, and naval—I reached our house. I sat on the terrace and started to spin my top as hard as I could. I don't know how much time I spent at it.

My mother finally saw me.

"Oh, so you're back."

"I came back by myself."

"Where is your father?"

"He's at work."

"He went to the consulate?"

"He's in the drains. He told me to tell you."

"*What?*"

My mother grabbed me and rushed out to the car, ordering me to show her which storm drain exactly Papa had gone into.

"*Finally!*" exclaimed my father the sewer man.

My mother couldn't drag him up by herself and asked some neighbors for help. One had the bright idea of bringing a rope, which he threw down into the *miso*. Strong arms lifted my father out. By this point a crowd of people had arrived and was watching the process with some interest. The sight was worth the detour. There are snowmen. Here was a mudman. And the smell wasn't uninteresting, either.

All the fuss made me understand that my father wasn't a drain-keeper after all, and that this had all been an accident. I felt a certain disappointment, not only because I had liked the idea of a member of my family having something to do with water, but also because, once again, I would have to figure out what "consul" meant.

I wasn't allowed to cross the street until after the floods.

■ ■ ■

WHEN IT RAINS INCESSANTLY, the ideal thing is do is swim. The antidote to water is lots of water.

Every day I went to Little Green Lake. Nishio-san took me, clutching tight to her umbrella—she was still on the side of the dry. As for me, of course, I had thrown myself into the opposite camp. I left the house in my swimsuit in order to get wet before swimming. The whole point was constant immersion.

I dove into the lake and stayed in. The best moment, as always, was when it poured. I would float on the surface, basking in the sublime shower. I

93

opened my mouth, accepting every drop offered. The universe was generous and I was thirsty enough to drink it all in.

Water beneath me, water above me, water in me—I was water. How appropriate that one definition of the Japanese character for my name was "rain." I, too, was precious and copious, inoffensive and deadly, silent and raucous, joyous and despicable, life-giving and corrosive, pure and grasping, patient and insidious, musical and off-key—but more than any of that, and beyond all those things, I was invulnerable.

Some might try to shield themselves from me by taking refuge under a roof or umbrella. That didn't bother me. I could permeate everything. Some might try and spit me out or channel me. I would find my way back in. I might even be found in the desert; at least I would come to mind there. Some might swear at me when I continued falling for the fourth straight day. I didn't care.

From the heights and depths of my diluvian life, I knew that I was rain and rain was rapture. Some realized it would be best to accept me, let me overwhelm them, let me be who I was. There was no greater luxury than to fall to earth, in sprinkles or in buckets, lashing faces and drenching countryside, swelling sources

and overflowing rivers, spoiling weddings and conse-
crating burials, the blessing and curse of the skies.

My rainy childhood thrived in Japan like a fish in
water.

Tired of my unending passion for my element,
Nishio-san would finally call to me,

"Out of the lake! You'll dissolve!"

Too late. I had dissolved long before.

* * *

AUGUST.

"*Mushiatsui*," complained Nishio-san. She was
right: it was as hot as a furnace. Liquefaction and sub-
limation took on a rhythm beyond most people's
endurance. My amphibious body delighted in it all.

My father found singing in this kind of heat hellish.
He hoped that the rain would force the outdoor Noh
performances to be canceled. I hoped so, too, not
only because the hours of Noh were crushingly dull,
but because of the joys inherent to the downpour.
Thunder rumbling in the mountains was the most
beautiful sound in the world.

I USED TO LOVE LYING TO MY SISTER. The best things were always made up.

"I have a donkey," I declared to her one day.

Why a donkey? I didn't know. I sometimes had no idea what would come out of my mouth from one second to the next.

"A donkey," I went on, "who is very brave."

"You're making this up."

"No, I have a real donkey. He lives on a prairie. I see him when I go to Little Green Lake."

"There isn't any prairie."

"It's a secret one."

"What's your donkey like?"

"He's gray, with long ears. His name is Kaniku."

"How do you know that's his name?"

"Because I gave it to him."

96

"You can't do that. He isn't yours."

"He is too mine."

"How do you know he doesn't belong to someone else?"

"He told me."

"Liar! Donkey's don't talk."

Rats. I had forgotten about that little detail. I pressed on nonetheless.

"He's a magic donkey who can talk."

"I don't believe you."

"Well too bad for you," I said haughtily.

I told myself that the next time I made up a story I would remember that animals don't talk.

I tried a new tack:

"I have a pet cockroach."

For reasons that escaped me, this lie didn't have any effect on my sister. I therefore decided to try telling the truth.

"I know how to read."

"Yeah, sure."

"But it's true."

"No it's not."

Okay, so the truth didn't work either. I continued my search for credibility:

"I'm three years old."

"Why are you always making things up?"

"I'm not lying. I *am* three."

"In ten days!"

"Okay, so I'm *almost* three years old."

" 'Almost' isn't the same. You're always telling lies."

I had to get used to the idea that I was not believable. Deep down, I didn't care whether or not I was believed.

I started telling stories. At least I believed them.

THE KITCHEN WAS EMPTY. It was not an occasion to be missed. I climbed up on the table and started to scale the north face of the pantry. Placing one foot on a box of tea, another on a packet of cookies, my hand gripping the cupboard handle, I neared the object I sought: the white metal container in which my mother hid the candy.

My goal was within reach. My heart started to race. My left foot braced on a sack of rice and my right on dried seaweed, I worked the lock and opened the container. Inside was treasure: chocolate doubloons, sugar pearls, chewing gum banknotes, liquorice diadems, and marshmallow bracelets. I was preparing to plant my flag and enjoy the view from atop this Everest of glucose when I heard footsteps.

Leaving my precious find at the top of the cupboard, I scrambled down and hid under the table. The feet arrived. I recognized Nishio-san's slippers and Kashima-san's *geta*.

The older woman sat down while the younger heated water for tea. Kashima-san, as usual, ordered Nishio-san around. Not content with that, she also told her horrible things.

"They despise you. That much is clear."

"That isn't true."

"Oh it's so obvious. The Belgian woman speaks to you as if you were her inferior."

"Only one person speaks to me as if I were an inferior. And that's you."

"Well, of course. That's because you are inferior. At least I'm not a hypocrite."

"*Madame* is not a hypocrite."

"You know, it's ridiculous the way you call her 'madame.'"

"She calls me Nishio-san, and in her language the equivalent is 'madame.'"

"When your back is turned, you can't be sure that she doesn't call you a maid."

"How would you know? You don't speak French."

"The whites have always despised the Japanese."

"These don't."

"Of course they do."

"*Monsieur* sings Noh!"

" *'Monsieur!'* Can't you see he does it to make fun of us?"

"He gets up every morning before dawn and goes to his lesson."

"It's normal that a soldier would get up early to defend his country's interests."

"He's a diplomat, not a soldier."

"And we saw what they did in nineteen forty-five, those 'diplomats.' "

"This is nineteen seventy."

"So what? Nothing has changed."

"If they are your enemies, why are you working for them?"

"I'm not working. Haven't you noticed?"

"I have noticed. Yet you take their money."

"It's nothing compared to what they owe us."

"They don't owe us anything."

"They took the most beautiful country in the world, and in nineteen forty-five they destroyed it."

"But we won in the end. Our country is richer than theirs now."

"Our country is not rich compared to what it was before the war. You didn't know what it was like then. There was reason to feel proud to be Japanese."

"You say that because you were young then. You're nostalgic."

"You don't have to talk about youth for something

to be beautiful. If you talked about yours it would be miserable."

"Yes, it would. That's because I was poor. My family was poor before the war as well."

"Before the war there was enough beauty for everyone, for poor people as well as rich."

"How would you know?"

"Today there's no beauty for anyone, rich or poor."

"Beauty is not hard to find."

"It is a fraction of what there once was. They have condemned it to disappear. That is Japan's decadence."

"I've heard this before."

"I know what you think. Even if you don't agree with me, you have good reason to be worried. You're not as loved here as much as you think. You're so naïve that you don't see the hate behind their smiles. That's as it should be. People of your sort are so used to being treated like dirt they don't even notice anymore. But I am an aristocrat, and I feel that they don't show me enough respect."

"You do get enough respect."

"Me they respect. I let them know that they shouldn't confuse me with you."

"And the result is that I'm part of the family and you are not."

"You're an idiot to think that."

"The children adore me, especially the little one."

"Well, of course she does! At that age they're like puppies. Give a puppy something to eat and it will love you."

"I love puppies."

"Listen, if you want to be a member of a family of dogs, that's your affair. But just don't be surprised to find if one day they start treating you like one."

"What are you saying?"

"You'll see," replied Kashima-san ominously, putting her bowl of tea down on the table, signaling the end of the discussion.

■ ■ ■

THE NEXT DAY Nishio-san told my father that she was leaving.

"I have too much work and I'm tired. I need to spend more time at home to take care of the twins. My daughters are ten, and they need me."

My parents were forced to accept her decision.

I wrapped my arms around Nishio-san's neck.

"Please don't go! Please!"

She wept but wouldn't change her mind. I saw Kashima-san smiling quietly.

I ran to my parents and managed to communicate what I had heard while hiding under the kitchen table. My father was furious with Kashima-san. He asked

Nishio-san to speak with him in private. I stayed in my mother's arms, sobbing and repeating over and over:

"Nishio-san has to stay with me! Nishio-san has to stay with me!"

Mama gently explained that, whatever happened, one day I would leave Nishio-san.

"Your father won't stay in Japan forever. In a year or two, or three, we will leave, and Nishio-san won't be coming with us. Maybe this is a good time for this to happen."

The universe was coming apart. I was being told so many abominations at once that I couldn't take any one of them in. My mother did not seem to understand that she was announcing the Apocalypse.

I struggled to formulate questions.

"We won't always stay here?"

"No. Your father will be posted somewhere else."

"Where?"

"We don't know."

"When?"

"We don't know that either."

"I'm not leaving here. I can't leave!"

"You don't want to live with us anymore?"

"Yes, I do, but you have to stay here too."

"We won't be allowed to stay."

"Why?"

"Because your father is a diplomat. That's his job."

"So what?"

"It means he has to do what Belgium tells him to do."

"Belgium is far away. It won't be able to punish him if he doesn't do what it says."

My mother laughed at this. I cried harder.

"You were teasing me! We're never going to leave, are we?"

"I wasn't teasing you. One day we will leave Japan."

"I can't leave! I have to live here! This is my country—and this is my house!"

"This isn't your country."

"Yes it is! If I leave I'll die!"

I began shaking my head like a lunatic. I was lost at sea and the waters were rising all around me. I fought against them, trying to gain a foothold, but there didn't seem to be one in sight. The world was finished with me.

"No, my darling, of course you won't die."

In a way I already had. I had just been told what at some point everyone learns: that eventually we lose what we love. *That which is given you will be taken back.* That was how I formulated the theme of my child-hood, of my adolescence, and of all the years that fol-lowed. *That which is given you will be taken back. Life will be punctuated by mourning—mourning for the country you love, for the mountain, the flowers, the house, Nishio-san, and the language. This is only the beginning of an endless series of losses. You will get none of them back, and find nothing to replace them, though there will be those who will try to console you, the way God consoles Job by "giving" him another wife, another home, other children. But you will be too smart to be fooled by this.*

"What did I do wrong?" I said, sobbing.

"You did nothing wrong. It is the way things are."

If only it had been my fault! Then at least this tragedy would be punishment. But this wasn't the case. It was the way things were. Being naughty or sweet didn't matter. *That which is given you will be taken back.* That is the rule.

At three we know we will someday die. Knowing that doesn't really mean anything. Dying is so far off that it is as if it will never happen. But learning at that age that in one, or two, or three years you will be thrown out of the garden, and without having disobeyed anyone, is the cruelest knowledge—the first of an infinite number of torments.

That which is given you will be taken back. If you only knew that someday someone will have the impudence to take you back.

I began howling.

At that moment my father and Nishio-san reappeared. She ran to me and swept me up in her arms.

"Don't worry, I'm staying! I'm not going to leave you!"

Had she told me this only a quarter of an hour earlier I would have exploded with joy. Now I knew this was only a reprieve. The tragedy would happen later.

Knowing what will happen in the future, we are faced with a simple choice: either we resolve not to become attached to people and things, or we decide to love them even more fiercely.

Because we don't have much time together, I will give you as much love in a year as I could give you in a lifetime.

That was my choice. I hugged Nishio-san tightly, with all the strength I had.

Kashima-san passed by and saw us—me in Nishio-san's arms, and Nishio-san looking contented and peaceful. She didn't know that I had overheard their conversation, but she sensed I had played some role in Nishio-san's decision to stay.

She pursed her lips and stared at me balefully.

. . .

MY FATHER TOLD ME that we wouldn't leave Japan for another two or three years. Even though that was an eternity to me, I would spend another lifetime in the land of my birth, this was bittersweet news, like medicine that eases the pain but doesn't cure the illness. I told my honorable father that perhaps he should change jobs.

He replied that he didn't think he wanted to work in the sewers.

From then on I became more solemn. The afternoon following the tragic revelation, Nishio-san took me to the playground. I spent an entire hour jumping madly on and off the edge of the sandbox repeating these words:

"You must remember! You must remember!"

However it was formulated in my child's imagination, what I meant was this:

You must remember because you will not always live in Japan, because you will be thrown out of the garden, because you will lose Nishio-san and the mountain, because that which is given you will be taken back. Memory has the same power as writing. When you see the word "cat" in a book, it looks very different from the neighbor's cat with the beautiful eyes. Yet to see the word written gives you a pleasure like the one the cat gave you when its golden gaze was fixed upon you.

Memory is like this. Your grandmother is dead but the memory of her makes her live. If you could write of the marvels of the paradise in your head, you would forever carry in your mind, if not their miraculous nature, then at least something of their power.

From now on you will lead a holy life. The moments will be draped in silks and crowned in the temple of your mind. Your emotions will be dynasties.

THE DAY OF MY THIRD BIRTHDAY came at last. This was the first birthday I could remember, and therefore the event seemed to me of cosmic importance. That morning I woke up believing that the entire village of Shukugawa had to be on holiday.

I jumped onto the bed of my sister, who was still asleep, and shook her.

"I want you to be the first to wish me happy birthday."

I thought she would think this a tremendous honor. "Happy birthday," she mumbled, and rolled over grumpily.

I left this ingrate and went down to the kitchen. Nishio-san was perfect. She knelt before the lord child that I was and congratulated me on my accomplishment. She was right. Not just anyone could turn three years. I felt an intense satisfaction.

I asked her if the people from the village would be coming to offer acclaim, or whether I needed to go out into the streets. The question confused Nishio-san for a moment, but she found a reply.

"It's summer," she said, "and almost everyone has left on vacation. Otherwise they would have organized a festival for you."

I told myself that perhaps this was for the best. The festivities would probably have been too much. My triumph would be best celebrated among my closest followers. The day's crowning moment would come when I was given the stuffed toy elephant.

My parents told me I would be given my present at teatime. Hugo and André informed me that they would refrain from teasing me for an entire day. Kashima-san said nothing.

I spent the hours in almost hallucinogenic impatience. The stuffed elephant would be the most fabulous present I would ever get. I wondered how long its trunk would be, and how heavy it would feel in my arms.

At four in the afternoon I was summoned to the table. I arrived with my heart pounding in my chest. I didn't see any packages. *They must have hidden them somewhere,* I thought.

There were the formalities, then cake—three candles that I quickly dispatched. We sang.

"Where is my present?"

My parents smiled slyly.

"It's a surprise."

That worried me.

"It isn't what I asked for?"

"It's better!"

Better than a velvety stuffed elephant? Impossible. Now I expected the worst.

"What is it?"

They led me out to the pool in the garden.

"Look in the water."

Three live carp were swimming around.

"We noticed that you love fish, and especially carp, so we bought you three. One for each year. Isn't that a wonderful idea?"

"Yes," I replied with determined politeness.

"One is orange, one is green, and one is silver. Aren't they beautiful?"

"Yes," I replied.

"You will take care of them. We bought lots of puffed rice cakes, and what you do is break them into pieces and throw them in the water—like that. Are you happy?"

"Yes."

I would rather have gotten nothing at all.

I WASN'T BEING POLITE to spare my parents' feelings. It was because no words could have expressed the intensity of my disappointment.

To the endless list of unanswerable questions must be added the following: why is it that well-intentioned parents, not content merely to foist an idea onto their child, also convince themselves that it was the child's idea in the first place?

People are often asked what, as children, they wanted to be when they grew up. In my case it would be better to ask my parents. Their replies would provide an idea of precisely what I *didn't* want to be when I grew up.

When I was three they announced "my" passion for fish. When I was seven they announced "my" decision to enter the Foreign Service. When I was twelve they were convinced I wanted to become a politician. And when I was seventeen, they declared that I would become the family lawyer.

I once asked them how they had arrived at their determinations about my future. They replied, with their usual aplomb, that "it was obvious," and that "everyone thought that." And when I asked them who "everyone" was, they said,

"Well, you know, *everyone*. For goodness sakes!"

There's no sense in fighting such conviction.

But back to my third birthday. As my mother and father had decided I would become a marine biologist, out of filial devotion I would do my best to mimic all the outward signs.

I started drawing fish with my crayons in my notebook—thousands of them: fish with big fins, little fins, multiple fins, green scales, red scales, blue scales with yellow polka dots, orange fish with purple stripes.

"What a good idea it was to give her those carp," said my parents, pleased with themselves.

*   *   *

THIS WHOLE STORY might have been comic had I not had to feed my new charges.

Every day, before lunch, I went into the pantry and took several cakes of puffed rice. Then, standing at the edge of the pool, I broke off sticky pieces about the size of popcorn and threw them into the water.

Actually, that part of it was sort of fun. The awful part was that these creatures rose to the surface to eat.

The vision of three disembodied mouths emerging from the water was unbearably revolting.

My parents, always full of good ideas, suggested we give the fish names.

"Your brother, your sister, and you—there are three of you, just like the carp," said my mother. "You could call the orange one André, the green one Juliette, and give the silver one your name."

"But that would make Hugo sad."

"Yes, that's true. Maybe we should buy you another carp."

Quick, I thought, *think of something. Anything!*

"But I've already given them names."

"Oh, I see. What do you call them?"

"Jesus, Mary, and Joseph."

"Jesus, Mary, and Joseph? Aren't those funny names for fish?"

"No."

"Which is which?"

"The orange one is Joseph, the green one is Mary, and the silver one is Jesus."

My mother laughed at the idea of a carp named "Joseph." My baptism was approved.

*　　*　　*

SO BEGAN THE DAILY ROUTINE. When the sun was directly overhead, I turned into the priestess of the fish. I blessed the rice cake, tore it into pieces, and cast them upon the water, saying, "This is my body that I give to you."

The gaping maws of Jesus, Mary, and Joseph appeared immediately, and in a great frenzy and thrashing threw themselves at the miserable stuff, fighting with each other over the last piece.

I wondered whether causing such a riot was really a good thing. I bit into one of the rice cakes. It tasted like wood pulp.

But these plump *saucisses* went crazy over this manna, which, when it became waterlogged, must have been truly horrible.

I tried not to look at their mouths. Watching people eat was bad enough, but nothing like how Jesus, Mary, and Joseph went at their food. A sewer pipe would have seemed a delicacy in comparison. The diameter of their mouths equaled that of their bodies. They looked like segments of tube except for those puffy fishy lips, which opened and closed with an obscene smacking noise—mouths shaped like life preservers that wanted to drown food and me with it.

I started feeding them with my eyes closed; otherwise I didn't think I could go through with it. I threw the pieces out into the water, and waited for the sucking and gurgling sounds to tell me that the trio had arrived, like a ravenous mob, having followed the alimentary trail. If I could have I would have put my hands over my ears.

In all my three years of life I had seen nothing as nauseating as this. I had looked intently at squashed frogs in the street, made pottery shapes out of my poop, examined closely the contents of my sister's handkerchief when she had a cold, and fearlessly poked my finger into a piece of raw veal—all motivated by genuine scientific curiosity—and felt not the slightest revulsion.

Why, then, did the mouths of carp cause me to break out in a cold sweat?

I had begun to think that our individuality lay in the following: tell me what disgusts you and I will tell you who you are. Our personalities mean nothing; our inclinations are mostly ordinary. What disgusts us expresses who we really are.

*　*　*

YEARS LATER, when I was learning Latin, I came across the phrase, *carpe diem*. As if by instinct I translated this into "a carp a day." This repugnant adage, if that's what it was, took me straight back to those days of torture at the side of the pool.

"Seize the day" is, of course, the right translation. Seize the day? What a joke. How could you enjoy anything before noon when all you thought about was the approaching session with these grotesque creatures, and then, after it was over, shuddered at the memory of it for the entire afternoon?

Not thinking about it was impossible. It would have

been like telling a Christian about to enter the Coliseum, "All you have to do is not think about the lion."

With each feeding, I got the growing feeling that it was my flesh the carp wanted. I began losing weight. After the fish had gobbled their lunch, I couldn't touch a bite of mine.

At night, in my bed, the darkness around me was filled with gaping mouths. I put my head under the pillow in terror and cried. I could feel their obese, scaly, writhing bodies under the covers with me, suffocating me—their cold, smacking lips moving all over me.

Jonah at least was lucky enough to be safely tucked away in the whale's stomach. Being swallowed by the carp wouldn't have been so bad. It wasn't their stomachs that terrified me, it was their mouths—the glottal vibrating of their mandibles sucking at me, night after interminable night. My nighttime visions were not of fairies and castles but of creatures from Hieronymus Bosch.

Related to this was the paralyzing fear that if I endured too many of their loathsome kisses I would turn into one of them. I would become cylindrical. My hands explored my body, expecting to find telltale signs of this dreaded metamorphosis.

TURNING THREE BROUGHT absolutely nothing good with it. The Japanese are right to see it as the end of the divine state. Something is lost, something more precious than anything and yet beyond recapture: belief in the goodness of the world.

I had heard my parents say that soon I would be going to a Japanese nursery school. I couldn't believe it. Leave my garden? Join a group of other children? What a ridiculous idea.

There would be worse. Something was amiss in the garden itself. Nature seemed to have reached a saturation point. The trees were too green, too leafy, the grass too lush, the flowers exploding as if they were engorged. By the middle of August, the plants began to look hungover. The vital force that I had sensed in the beginning had given way to an overripe heaviness.

Without knowing it, I was being shown one of the most terrifying laws of the universe: what doesn't advance retreats. First comes growth and then decay, and between the two is a void. There is no such thing as an apogee—it's an illusion—and therefore there is no real summer. Instead, there's a long spring, a spectacular leap of sap and yearning, and, once this is over, fall has begun.

After August 15, death seized the day. Though the leaves showed no sign of turning, the trees were full as ever, the vegetation no less profuse, and the garden beds prospered, nature was entering a golden age, even if there really isn't such a thing as a golden age because there is no stasis.

At the age of three I knew nothing of all this. I was still living the glory years of the king who, on his deathbed, cries, "That which must end has already ended." I would have been incapable of formulating the terms of my pain, but O how keenly I sensed the impending doom. Nature was trying too hard, and that meant it was hiding something.

Had I asked anyone they might have explained the cycle of seasons to me. At the age of three you don't remember the year before, so you don't have any sense of the eternal return. Every new season seems irreversible.

At the age of two, you don't notice these changes and you don't care. At four, you notice them but the memory of the year before takes the drama out of them. But at three, the anxiety you feel is overwhelming, because you see everything and understand nothing. There is no legal precedent to consult. You don't automatically ask adults questions, for you're not yet convinced that they have more wisdom. Perhaps that's not wrong.

At three, you're like an alien, equally fascinated and terrified by what you find. Everything is opaque and new. You must invent laws based upon your own observation. You have to be little Aristotle twenty-four hours a day, and this is particularly exhausting because you've never even heard of Aristotle.

One robin does not make it spring. At three, you would love to know how many robins it takes to mean anything. One dying flower does not make it fall, nor do two. Nonetheless, a feeling of unease sets in. How many wilting flowers does it take before an alarm goes off in your head, signaling that death is coming?

Aware that life was changing, I took refuge in my spinning top, as if it had critical information to impart. If only I could understand what it said.

THE END OF AUGUST. Noon. Time for my martyr-dom.

Don't be afraid, I told myself. *You have done it before and survived. You can get through this.*

I took the rice cakes from the pantry and went to out to the pool. The sun made the water sparkle like aluminum foil. I knew this brilliant, smooth surface would soon be spoiled by Jesus, Mary, and Joseph. Joseph had jumped, which was their way of calling each other for lunch.

When they had finished pretending to be flying fish (which, given their girth, was particularly obscene), they opened their mouths wide on the surface of the water and waited.

I threw the pieces of rice cake. They lunged for the pieces, sucking them down their tubes. Once they had eaten they clamored for more, opening their jaws so wide that I could see all the way down to their stomachs. While I dispensed their pitiful allotment I became more and more obsessed by what these carp were revealing to me. Normally, creatures concealed the interiors of their bodies. What would it be like, I wondered, if people displayed their insides?

The carp were breaking a primordial taboo: exposing their digestive tracts to the world.

You find that repugnant? That's what your stomach is like, too. If this obsesses you so much maybe it's because you see your reflection. Don't you know that this is what people are like? They may eat less greedily, but they eat, and the insides of your mother and your sister are exactly the same.

You think you're different? You're a tube who emerged from a tube. Lately you've had some grand sense of being different, of having greater thoughts. Fool. You're a tube and a tube is all you will ever be.

I silenced this voice telling me such horrors. Each day at noon for two long weeks I had faced these fish and their mouths, and rather than getting used to it I had become more and more depressed. What if feeding them was more than just some gross thing I had to do, but a divine message? Were that the case, to understand what it meant I had to let the voice speak.

Open your eyes. Life is what you see: the membrane, the guts, the bottomless hole that demands to be filled. Life is a tube that swallows and remains empty.

My feet were poised at the edge of the pool. I regarded them suspiciously, as if suddenly they weren't to be trusted. My eyes looked around at the garden. No longer was it my shield from the outside world, my perfect little paradise. It harbored death.

Which are you going to choose? Life—the gobbling, slab-bering mouths of carp—or death—slow vegetal putrefaction? What makes you least nauseous?

I couldn't think any longer. I shivered. My eyes looked down at the gaping mouths. I was cold. I retched. My legs couldn't support me. I stopped fighting and, hypnotized, collapsed into the pool.

My head struck the stone edge. The pain vanished almost as soon as I felt it. Independent of my commands, my body rolled over, stretched out horizontally, then sank halfway to the bottom, coming to a floating halt three feet down. Everything became calm again.

How strange it seemed. The last time I had drowned I had been enraged. I had felt an overwhelming desire to get back to the surface. Not this time. This time I had made a choice. I didn't even miss the air.

Feeling deliciously serene, I looked at the sky. Again the sunlight had never seemed so beautiful as it did from under water.

I felt at home. I had never felt better. Seen from this liquid perspective the world was quite wonderful. So completely had the water absorbed me that I didn't make a ripple. Upset by my intrusion, the carp had scampered to the far side of the pool and remained motionless. The water grew still, allowing me to observe clearly the trees in the garden, as if through a gigantic monocle. I chose to look only at the bamboo near the water's edge; nothing in this universe so deserved to be admired as bamboo. The three feet of water that separated me from them intensified their beauty.

I smiled with happiness.

Suddenly something came between the bamboo and me—the silhouette of someone leaning over the water. I thought with irritation that this person would want to take me out.

The prism of the water gradually revealed the person's features. It was Kashima-san. I was no longer afraid. She wouldn't intervene. She was a true Japanese. Moreover, she hated me.

I was right. Kashima-san's elegant face remained impassive. She looked me in the eyes. Could she see that I was happy? I don't know. No one can know what goes on in the mind of a Japanese from the old days.

One thing was certain. This woman would let me die.

I knew that one day we would understand one another, Kashima-san. Everything is fine now. When I was drowning in the sea and I was watching the people on the beach watching me it made me sick. But now because of you I understand them. They were as calm as you are. They didn't want to disturb the law of the universe, which

*is demanding that I drown. They had known that saving
me served no purpose. She who must drown will drown.
My mother took me out of the water and here I am back
in it.*

It seemed to me that Kashima-san was smiling.

*You're right to smile. When one's destiny is fulfilled, one
should smile. I'm happy to know that I will never have to
feed the carp again. And that I will never leave Japan.*

Now I saw it clearly: Kashima-san was smiling. At
long last she had smiled at me! Then she moved
slowly away.

Dying takes time. It felt as if I had been floating
between the waters for an eternity. I thought again
about Kashima-san. There is nothing more fascinating
than the facial expression of someone watching you
die. She could easily have lifted a little girl out of a
pool. But had she done that, she would not have been
Kashima-san.

What a relief it was that I would never again have
to be afraid of death.

⁂

IN 1945, ON OKINAWA, an island off the south
coast of Japan, something—I don't know what word
to use—happened.

It took place shortly after the surrender. The
island's inhabitants knew that the war was over and

that the Americans, who had already landed, would soon take over. They also knew that the latest orders were to stop resisting.

That was all they knew. Earlier their leaders had assured them that the Americans would kill every last Japanese. The inhabitants of Okinawa still believed this. As the white soldiers advanced, the Japanese retreated. Eventually they reached the end of the island, where steep cliffs plunged into the sea. Persuaded that they were going to be killed anyway, most of them leaped to their death.

The cliffs are very high, and below them the shore is covered with sharp rocks. Not one of those who jumped survived. When the Americans arrived, they were horrified by what they discovered.

I went to see these cliffs in 1989, and there was nothing, not even a tiny sign, to indicate what had happened there. Within a matter of hours thousands of people had committed suicide in this place, and it was unchanged. The sea had swallowed up the bodies broken on the rocks and left behind no trace of them. In Japan, suicide by drowning is more common than seppuku.

You can't visit this spot on Okinawa without trying to put yourself in the place of those who leaped. Some may have been afraid of being tortured. The beauty of the setting may have encouraged others to commit an act that, to them, was the highest expression of patriotism.

Nonetheless, one truth about this hecatomb seems inescapable: from the top of these great cliffs thousands killed themselves to avoid being killed; thousands died because they were afraid of death. The paradox staggers the mind.

It isn't really a matter of approving or disapproving, as if that would do the dead any good. But I can't help thinking that the true reason for committing suicide is fear of dying.

* * *

AT THREE, ONCE AGAIN, I knew nothing of all that. I knew only that I wanted to die in the carp pool. The great moment was coming because I could see my life unraveling. I couldn't manage to see the details. It was like being on an express train going so fast that you can't read the names of the little stations whizzing past. It didn't matter. I was enveloped by a delightful absence of pain.

"It" was beginning to overwhelm the "I" that had been serving me for the previous six months. It felt itself turning back into the tube that perhaps it had never stopped being in the first place. At long last, disencumbered of all its other useless functions, it was open to water—and to nothing else.

A HAND SEIZED the dying thing by the nape of the neck and shook "it" brutally back to "I."

Air entered my lungs, taking back command of the bronchial tubes. The pain was intense. I screamed. I was alive. I could see. Nishio-san.

She screamed for help. She was alive, too. She ran into the house with me in her arms and found my mother, who took one look at me and screamed as well.

"We're going to Kobe Hospital!"

Nishio-san accompanied us, running, all the way to the car. In a combination of Japanese, French, English, and loud groans, she was babbling to my mother about how she had found me.

My mother threw me onto the back seat and sped off, driving like a madwoman, which truly is an absurd thing to do when you're trying to save someone's life. She started telling me what must have happened.

"You were feeding the fish and you slipped. You fell into the water. Normally that would have been okay because you can swim, but when you fell you hit your head on the rocks at the bottom and you knocked yourself out."

I was perplexed. I knew perfectly well what had happened.

"Do you understand?" she asked me.

"Yes."

I understood that I must not tell her the truth. I understood that it was better to hold to this official version. Besides, I didn't know what words to use to tell her what had happened. I didn't know the word "suicide."

There was something, however, that I did wish to say.

"I don't want to feed the carp again!"

"Of course—yes—I understand. You're afraid you'll fall in the water again. I promise you. You'll never have to feed them again."

Well, at least I had that. My action hadn't been in vain.

"I will hold you in my arms and we'll feed them together."

I closed my eyes. Everything would start over again.

* * *

MY MOTHER CARRIED ME into the emergency room.

"You have a hole in your head," she told me.

Now that was news. I was delighted. I wanted to know more about it.

"Where is it?"

"On the side of your head. Where you hit the bottom."

"Is it a big hole?"

"Yes. You're losing lots of blood."

She put her fingers against my temple and showed me that they were covered with blood. Fascinated, I put my own finger in the wound, not caring that this might reveal how crazy I was.

"It's torn."

"Yes, your skin is open."

I looked at my blood, delighted with it.

"I want to look in the mirror! I want to see the hole in my head!"

"Calm down, calm down."

The nurses took over and reassured my mother. I couldn't hear what they were saying. I was thinking about the hole in my head. They wouldn't let me see it, so I had to imagine it. I saw my skull with a hole on the side. This was ecstasy.

I put my finger back there, because I wanted to explore what was inside, but a nurse gently took my hand and stopped me.

"They're going to sew up your head," said my mother.

"With a needle and thread?"

"Something like that."

I don't remember whether or not they put me to sleep. I believe I can still see the doctor standing over me, stitching up my temple with a thick black thread and a needle, like a tailor working on a suit.

* * *

AND SO CAME to an end my first and—to this day—
only suicide attempt.

I never told my parents that what happened was
not an accident.

Nor did I ever tell them about Kashima-san, and
what she had done, or not done. That would have
caused her some problems. She hated me and must
have been delighted at my approaching death.
Nonetheless, I still feel there's the chance that she
understood the true nature of what I was doing, and
had respected my choice.

Did I feel disappointed that I was still alive? Yes.
Was I also glad to have been taken from the waters in
time? Yes. I had chosen indifference. At bottom, it
was all the same to me, being alive or being dead. It
was only a question of time.

Even today I can't decide. Would it have been better had my life ended in August of 1970, in the pool
of carp? How can I know? I have found life to be very
interesting, but how can I know whether the other
side might not be more interesting?

It doesn't really matter. We will eventually find
out. And, when death comes, even the best-inten-
tioned people in the world won't be able to help us.

What I remember most clearly is how at home I felt between the waters.

Sometimes I wonder if I didn't simply dream all this—or just make it up. Then I look at myself in the mirror, and I see on my left temple the admirably eloquent scar.

* * *

AFTER THAT, nothing more happened.